Fairytales Written by Rabbits

Fairytales Written by Rabbits

Mary A Parker

Ferox Publishing
Melbourne, Australia

*For all creatures of the Big Ears Animal Sanctuary,
with two legs or four.*

*All author royalties earned from the sale of this
book will be donated to the Big Ears Animal
Sanctuary, Tasmania.*

*With special thanks to all those who offered
support and encouragement on this project.*

Contents

When men are fairy tales in books
written by rabbits.

The dust came in the late evening, many seasons ago.
Flashes of light flowed and danced across the twilight sky.
Green, orange and purple streaks twisted among the clouds

and stars. The rabbits were frightened at first, fleeing to the familiar darkness of their burrows, away from the unknown.

Only a brave few emerged to stare at the spectacle, like nothing they'd ever seen. They watched the colours fade and fall from the sky as fine dust, settling over the surrounding landscape from one horizon to the other.

The strange dust settled on trees, grass and the bold rabbits themselves who had dared to venture forth. It glittered on their fur and frosted their whiskers.

The rabbits looked around in wonder. No rabbit had wondered before.

But first they must catch you.

The long, dry summer dragged on forever. Heath crouched on the hillside in the shade cast by the Eucalypt that grew at its peak. The ancient tree littered the surrounding ground with dry, brittle leaves. Parched, unappetising grass grew to heights high above his head. Older rabbits had told him that many summers were like this, though he'd not yet lived to learn this for himself. He was only a young rabbit, well grown but as yet inexperienced. His speckled grey-brown fur hid him well in the shadows of the grass, where he stretched out in the dirt, trying to keep cool.

This warren was home. He lived here with a great extended family of parents, many uncles, aunts, cousins and siblings. Most of his cousins would wander away as they grew, searching for other warrens to call their home. He supposed he would too, one day. However, until that day came, the furthest he'd wander was to the meager pool of water by the stone burrow. The world beyond that waited for him was an unknown, frightening idea, and he was in no hurry to face it.

His ears swivelled towards the sound of someone hopping tentatively towards him. A few paces, then a rest, no doubt inspecting the sky for hawks, before continuing towards him. His whiskers twitched at the familiar scent.

"Brother?" whispered Millet, edging closer through the tall grass, "Are you there?"

"I'm here," he replied, lifting his head so he'd be easier to see. She hopped over delicately, and the siblings sniffed each other in greeting. Though born in the same litter, she was smaller than her brother, more delicate and still round in the face. Her soft fur was more brown than grey and she'd not yet had a growth spurt like him. She hadn't yet grown a dewlap and in many ways still resembled a kit rather than the adult she would be expected to be. She was so petite that she hardly left imprints in the dust where she hopped.

"Are you going to the water?" she asked. Her lips were as dry as the soil in her coat. Little moisture remained in the grass of late, so increasingly the rabbits had to make the exposed journey to the little water that remained at the stone burrow. "I wanted to wait," he replied, "It smells like rain is coming." Heath, by contrast, had grown rapidly and grown well, with new found strength that made some of his uncles nervous. He was long and athletic, already as large as the other bucks that had travelled from distant warrens, like Bracken and Flax. The other bucks had a few months growth ahead of Heath, but he easily matched them physically. Several of the Elder Rabbits had begun saying it was time for him to find a new warren. Heath wondered whether that was because of his growth, or because of the difficult questions he liked to ask. "Please, I can't wait," she whispered, crouching low to the ground. "I'm so thirsty. Please go with me?" Heath rubbed noses with his sister.

"Okay, if you can't wait, we'll go to the water."

The two rabbits travelled cautiously, sprinting one at a time from one scraggly bush another. They frequently glanced at the sky for hawks and always listening for the ever present danger of a fox.

The lives of rabbits had changed since the night the dust fell from the sky, generations ago. Before that night, rabbits hadn't spent time contemplating the future, or the distant past. The rabbits from before the sky dust fell believed the world was the same now as it had always been. Now, however, the world was different. The rabbits themselves were different. Each generation asked more questions than the last. The Elders worried that these younger rabbits were spending too much time with questions, and not enough time being a rabbit. Some Elders even worried that their Elders, long dead, never even thought to worry about the younger generation. They'd have never even considered the absurd possibility that a rabbit might somehow be not rabbit enough. Perhaps they didn't know how. Both possibilities seemed equally troublesome to the Elders. They discouraged young rabbits like Heath from worrying about such things and instead told to focus on their survival and the imminent threat of being eaten.

The stone burrow, was the last place water still gathered in the parched landscape. It had simply always been, since the day rabbits first shared stories, but nobody understood how it had come to exist. The burrow was dug out of hard grey stone, harder than any normal rabbit could dig. Its entrance stood so high that ten or more rabbits could stand on each others shoulders and not touch the top. At the entrance was more grey stone, flat so the water gathered upon it. The rabbits needed to climb down steep, exposed banks of the same pale, grey stone to reach the remaining water. One of the exposed banks had crumbled, so rabbits would scamper down the gravel, dirt and debris to reach the water with little difficulty. The smooth stone inclines were extremely difficult to climb when dry, and would be impossible when wet.

At first, rabbits had been afraid of the stone burrow. They wondered what kind of creature must have dug it, to be so big and strong to dig through stone. They worried that it might return, that it might desire to eat them, and so they watched the burrow warily from a distance. But as the summer drew on, and other water sources vanished, necessity meant that the rabbits had to face the stone burrow. With no other water source to rely upon the rabbits had little choice but to venture down to the exposed pool for their infrequent drink.

One day, out of necessity, the rabbits wondered if they didn't need to fear it. Perhaps it was placed there just for them, so they would continue to have water when other sources failed. The legend of the Great Stonecutter Rabbit was born, a giant that dug through rock and hills so that a little water would still flow to the rabbits. It was a gift, and worthy of respect instead of fear.

Caution, however, was still justified. The mouth of the burrow was open and exposed with only a single exit. A rabbit could easily be cornered down there on her own by a fox or a hawk. Long-living rabbits were cautious rabbits. Heath crept up to the edge of the incline from downwind, sniffing the air, ears pricked for the slightest sound that might reveal a threat before it was too late. All he heard was the ever present buzzing of fat, lazy blowflies that seemed omnipresent in the sweltering heat.

"I think it's safe," he whispered, never taking his eyes off the clearing, "I'll keep watch." Millet nodded and crept her way around the rim of the stone banks, pausing to lift her head and sniff the wind as she went. She delicately navigated her way down the debris, sliding a little on the gravel onto the scorching stone below. She froze, crouched into the gravel and dirt waiting to see if the noise attracted any attention.

Heath looked around, but still they were alone except for the flies. Millet hoped slowly to the edge of the water, disturbing the insects that also drank there, and began lapping greedily at the small pool.

Heath dutifully kept watch. It was probably far too hot for a fox to be hunting now, if it was sensible, but hunger did strange things to a creature. His mind wandered briefly to the stone burrow and the great creature that must have dug it. *What would it look like? How would it smell?*

Millet sat up and shook her head, a few drops of precious water spattering from her whiskers and startling the flies. She glanced up at her brother, still keeping watch though his mind had wandered, before attempting to climb back. Heath watched her struggle up the rubble, choosing her path carefully lest she make more slide down, and eventually reach the top, panting. She scampered back to her brother, short of breath, and earnestly began to clean her damp feet. They'd already begun to dry in the brief moments it had taken her to climb back up to him.

"Do you feel better?" he asked her, scanning the surrounds for danger once more.

"Yes, thank-you," she replied, still panting slightly. "I was so dry, I couldn't wait."

"Rest a moment," he suggested, "Then we'll go back." Millet flopped onto the ground in the shade of the grass, lying on her side to expose her white belly. A breeze rustled the grass, still too warm to bring any relief. Heath glanced again at the sky, clouds slowly rolling in from the horizon.

"Will all summers be this hot?" Millet sighed, allowing herself a moment of rest and shutting her eyes briefly. Heath contemplated this for a moment.

"How can I know?" he asked. "The Elders say that every summer is the hottest. Perhaps they get hotter each time."

"Then we're doomed," Millet muttered. "If it's any hotter, there wont be any water left next summer."

"Or perhaps," Heath offered another thought, "Perhaps the summer of now is always the hottest, when we remember the summers of the past." Millet glanced up at him from where she lay.

"The Elders wouldn't like to hear you speak that way," she reminded him. He licked his front legs, hoping the little moisture would help him to cool down.

"Don't remind me," he grumbled, "But how can I change how I think?" Millet pulled herself to her feet and shook the dust once more from her fur.

"Will you be leaving soon?" she asked. "For another warren? For a mate?" Heath started down the path back towards the warren and the Great Eucalypt, Millet following a few steps behind him.

"I don't know," he admitted. "Everything beyond the warren seems so big and far away. I would miss being here so much."

"To be honest, I would miss you being here too," she confessed. They continued picking their way carefully from cover to cover back to the warren. Familiar tracks and scats marked the well worn trails home. By now dark grey clouds had blown in overhead. The wind was picking up strength, rustling the grass of its own accord and blowing fine dirt into the rabbits' faces. They saw the Great Eucalypt of the warren ahead, its scraggly branches swaying in the growing squall, dislodging more parched leaves. Millet stood up on her hind legs, sniffing the wind, fur bristling.

"Something's wrong," she cried. Heath raised himself up beside her for a better view. He scanned the terrain in front of them. Other rabbits ahead of them bolted for their holes as refuge from the weather. He too felt uneasy.

"I don't see it," he confessed. *How can you warn the others of a danger if you don't know where it is?*

"Nor I," his sister replied, "But it's here." She glanced around, chose a craggy rock to climb and raised herself up again to her full height for a better look. Heath cringed. She was so exposed in that position. Whatever the danger they were sensing was, it would surely notice her up there. His fur prickled.

Suddenly the clouds tore open with a deafening roar and a flash like the midday sun. Startled, Millet fell from her vantage point and scrambled to her feet.

"What was that?" she gasped, eyes wide with fear. Heath forced himself to be brave and looked up at the sky as another roar and flash lit up the landscape.

"It's the sky," he breathed back. "The sky is angry." His little heart beat wildly in his chest, like a butterfly trying to escape a spider's web.

"We need to get home," he urged his sister. She was almost paralysed with fear. He nudged her, gently at first, to start moving, then with increasing force. She shook herself to her senses and began to sprint for the warren, with complete disregard for cover. Heath followed, trying desperately to suppress the urge to outrun her, in case she didn't make it without him.

Without warning, the sky lit up once more and an arc of light darted erratically through the clouds to strike a branch of the Great Eucalypt. Heath and Millet skidded to a halt, wide eyed. The struck branch glowed with rapidly growing flame.

"What's happening?" cried Millet, panting heavily.

"Something awful," Heath replied. They stared, unsure what to do, as the flames licked their way from one branch to another. The crown of the Eucalypt was rapidly being consumed in the orange glow of the fire. He crouched low, trying to force his panicked mind to think, to have a plan, an escape route. All the burrows were closer to the fire, they couldn't go there.

"Oh no!" Millet whispered. He followed her gaze to watch one of the Eucalypt's burning branches creak and fall under the strain of the wind and fire, dragging burning leaves with it. It landed with a crash, but the noise was drowned out by the ongoing storm. Almost instantly, the tinder dry grasses around the warren began to burn. Embers caught the wind, drifting on cruel zephyrs and landed a few metres closer to the petrified rabbits. Heath thumped on the ground with his powerful legs, a warning for anyone that might listen.

"Run!" he screamed. "Run away!" He turned to flee, and caught his sister's gaze, the burning tree and grass surrounding the warren reflected in her wide eyes.

"Where?" she gasped, on the brink of panic.

"Anywhere!" he replied, darting past her, flashing his tail,

"Anywhere away!" He bolted downwind. Already the sound of the flames crackled in his ears. She ran after him, sheer terror the only reason she kept pace.

He reached the top of another rise before he dared look behind him. The Eucalypt was well and truly ablaze. Streaks of flame spread out from the tree. Embers fluttered in the wind, rising up and then falling in new areas of flammable grass. Small skinks scurried out of the way, seeking futile shelter under rocks nearby. Movement caught his eye in the sky above. Squinting against the wind and smoke, he scanned the clouds. Millet finally caught up with him.

"Not that too," he muttered. Again, lightning lit up the sky, highlighting the silhouette of a hawk circling above. He desperately wanted to be under cover, but didn't know where would be safe with the oncoming fire. Millet, panting heavily beside him, tried to catch her breath.

"We need to be upwind," she said, "I think we need to get to the other side." Heath wasn't really listening; he was too preoccupied staring at the hawk as it dived towards the warren. The hawk rose on the hot air from the flames again, clutching not a rabbit in its talons, but a glowing stick.

"What does it want with that?" Heath wondered out loud. He'd never even heard of such behaviour from a hawk. But the flicker of curiosity quickly turned to a wave of dread as the hawk sailed closer, and dived towards them, burning stick still in its talons.

"R-run!" Millet stammered. The two rabbits bolted, zigzagging through the grass, old instincts seizing control of their minds. Grass rustled behind him, and suddenly the hawk was there, in his peripheral vision, the burning stick spreading its flames in the grass behind him. The black hawk dropped the stick and began to rise. Embers greedily caught hold of the fine, dry grasses and turned to flames.

"You're mine, runner," it hissed as it rose on the hot air. *It knows*, Heath thought, *it knows exactly what it's doing.* He felt the growing heat behind him; saw his own shadow in front of him cast by the flickering flames.

"Run straight!" he screamed for his sister. "It's spreading the fire!"

Heath stopped his erratic movements. If the hawk had wanted to it would have already struck him by now. He sprinted in a straight line to distance himself from the new fire as rapidly as possible. The air in his lungs felt like it was already burning, and his leg muscles were aching, only adrenaline keeping them from collapse. The whole world smelt of smoke and sweat and fear, but his only option was to move, to run. To run like only rabbits ran. There was no time for thinking.

Then Millet appeared beside him. He didn't know if she'd always been there, or if they'd split and reunited. His sister looked as exhausted as he did, sweat soaking her sides with precious water. She looked up, taking her eyes off the path in front of her for a mere moment, and tripped. Her little body rolled nose over tail before collapsing in a heap.

"Come on!" Heath skidded to a halt. "Get up!" He looked back, allowing himself only a moment to watch her rise, all the while fear screaming at him to *RUN RUN RUN*. She rose, barely, to her feet, trembling.

"It's in front," she moaned sorrowfully, "The hawk's in front!" Heath glanced around in time to see the black hawk rising from the vegetation ahead, and the growing light of more fire. He could hear it crackling. It was so fast! How could they ever be faster? He turned downwind, the only direction that didn't yet glow with heat.

"This way!" he urged his sister, "Quickly!" He dared not wait to see if she followed, racing with the wind at his back, flashing his white tail in fright. He needn't have worried for her, in a moment she was beside him again, running together. The way ahead was clear, the path behind growing ever hotter and filling with dark smoke. He ran so hard he thought his legs would fall off, or his racing heart would beat out of his body and fly ahead of him. Somehow he kept up with himself.

Instinct made him glance over his shoulder. Against the glowing backdrop of the fire, the hawk was diving towards them, no stick in its talons this time. This time he meant to catch them. This would all be over very soon.

Millet was behind him. She was the smaller of the two. She was the easier target. This would soon be over for her.

No, thought the un-rabbit-like thoughts, the ones that upset the Elders. *It doesn't have to be.* They jostled for space in his mind, tried to suppress the mad fear with cunning, with a plan. He slowed down, let her overtake him but kept pace to stay only a few body lengths behind her. Her white tail flashed in front of him as she sped away. Now, he was sure, he would be the target. He hoped, if this mad plan didn't work, if she actually survived to think about it later, that she would realise what he had done.

The path ahead was clear, enough for him to be sure of his footing. He glanced over his shoulder, and felt like the whole world slowed down, just for him.

The black hawk was there, in a dive, talons outstretched to grab him. Powerful flight muscles shielded its chest; the piercing beak gaped ready and hungry in front of golden eyes, completely focused on him. There was only one chance. At speed, moments from impact, Heath crouched on his front and kicked up with his powerful hind legs. Heath tumbled, white tail flashing over his head. He stole a glance behind him through his font paws to see the hawk within reach, its talons striking the ground where his hindquarters had been. Every detail of the hawk was highlighted in his vision, every pattern on its singed feathers, every scale of its feet. He kicked up at the height of his tumble and felt with terror the scrape of the beak on his back before his feet collided with the hawk's neck. The hawk collapsed, dragging Heath with it by its grip on his left hip. Heath kicked again, and again, raking his claws through the feathered neck and around the head. Sharp pain coursed through his body as the curved beak dug into his thigh. The hawk flapped, bringing up its wings and talons, no longer going for the kill, but attempting to defend itself. Ahead, his sister shrieked. The hawk cursed and finally let go, and Heath sprinted away with all his remaining speed, pain throbbing in his leg.

He couldn't see his sister. He couldn't see very much, smoke clouded his vision and choked his lungs. *Where is she? Is there a second hawk? She can't be far.*

Suddenly he found himself falling, tumbling uncontrollably down a grey stone slope to crash at the mouth of the stone burrow.

"Brother!" Millet was there, crouching petrified in the water, watching the sky. There was no cover here, only the meager pool of water and the dark gaping mouth of the stone burrow. His body aching, he pulled himself to his feet and limped over. Over the lip of the stone edge, the hawk took to the sky once more.

"It's no good," he panted, "We can't outrun them." His eyes were watering from the billowing smoke. He gasped for air, but his breaths weren't enough to satisfy his lungs.

"There's nowhere to hide," Millet cried. She looked exhausted. She might collapse with fright any moment now. He looked behind her, to the dark gaping mouth of the burrow. No rabbit before had entered beyond the first few metres. None had dared.

"There's one place," he said, nudging her to turn around. "We don't have a choice." She turned to look at the burrow, then glanced up at the sky. The storm clouds glowed orange with the reflected light of the fire.

"No," she agreed, and scampered into the darkness, "We don't." He limped after her, hoping that if there was a Great Stonecutter Rabbit somewhere in this burrow, that it would be understanding and not hungry.

Outside, finally, it began to rain.

Take me with you stream, far, far
away.

The air in the burrow was surprisingly cool, moistened by
the slow, ever-present trickle of water. The two rabbits crept
cautiously ever deeper into the burrow, climbing part way up
the eerily perfect round walls to avoid their feet getting wet.

Ahead of them lay pure darkness, only the faint glow of the fires outside lit the path behind them. Though no longer in danger from the hawk or the flames, Heath felt no calmer. The unknown was just as frightening, and the faint breeze carried unfamiliar scents from deep within the burrow. He smelled no evidence of a rabbit having been here before. He wasn't sure what he could smell, but it was better than the choking smoke.

Heath's whole body ached from exertion and fear. His wounded haunches stung, but the rabbits dared not stop and dared not go back.

"Will the others be alright?" Millet asked after a while, to break the silence.

"I don't know," Heath replied. In truth he didn't have any idea how they could possibly be alright, between the fire and the opportunistic hawk. All he could really hope for was that the heat of the flames hadn't reached the deepest burrows, but he didn't know how likely that hope might be. Even if they'd fled, the hawk had been spreading the fire deliberately to trap them. It was certain that somebody had died today, he just couldn't be sure who, or if it might have been everybody. Millet stopped and sat up. He couldn't see her expression in the dark, but she sounded worried under the fatigue.

"Should we go back?"

Heath sat down for a moment to think. If they went home, what would be waiting for them? The hawk? The fire? The burnt hollow of the once mighty Eucalypt? Was it possible anyone had even survived? How had such a thing happened? "I don't know," he replied. "I really don't." Millet hunched down beside him. Drenched in sweat, she'd cooled rapidly in the stone burrow.

"We don't really know much, do we?" she observed. "At least it's cool in here. I can barely remember being cool." Heath crept forward to the trickle of water in the middle of the burrow and lapped slowly. He hadn't realised just how parched his mouth had become during the run and spluttered initially.

"Do you think the Great Stonecutter Rabbit is real?" Millet asked him. "Do you think he'll mind that we're in his burrow?" Heath coughed some dust from his throat.

"I don't know if he's real," he replied, "but this burrow is real, and it's dug through stone. Something did this because it's here now. And we're very lucky it is."

His throat finally clear, he allowed himself to drink. The slow trickle of water flowed back the way they had come. Once he would have thought of the way back home as the way back to safety, to the familiar and comfortable. Now, no matter whether they chose to go forward or back, both directions would take them into the unknown.

"What do you think we'll find?" Millet asked, looking deeper into the burrow. There was no light ahead, but her soft voice echoed off the cold stone. Her questions repeated as they faded away.

"That's another thing I don't know," Heath replied.

"The Stonecutter Rabbit must be a giant," Millet marvelled, her fear fading to give way to wonder. "His burrow is so big. Maybe he'll be so big that he won't notice we're here." She skipped forward a few steps, peering into the darkness.

"Maybe he won't be home, and we'll find his den where he sleeps. I wonder if his fur is rough like the stone." She paused for a moment, ears pricked forward, listening to her own echoes, mimicking her curiosity.

"Maybe," Heath replied between mouthfuls of water. Millet hopped back towards him.

"Or maybe he has other exits, and we'll come up above ground far away. Maybe there'll be a new warren, or more giant rabbits, or something else that I can't even imagine."

"We'll whatever is up there, there's water that way," Heath replied after he finished drinking. "And where there's water, there's grass, and that's good enough for me." He stretched, readying himself for what he suspected may be a long journey.

"Let's keep going." His sister nodded, though he barely saw her movements in the dark. They pressed on down the burrow, Millet a few paces ahead of her brother, who found himself slowing as the pain in his hip worsened. Heath consoled himself in the fact that at least he was still able to walk. There were much worse injuries he could have received from the hawk. He only heard the echoes of their feet, nails clicking against stone, and the tiny trickle of water.

"I'm sure whatever we find on the other side will be good," Millet chirped. She waited for him to catch up to her. He stopped when his whiskers brushed against hers.

"What makes you say that?"

"Well, this stone burrow was meant for us," she replied. "It has lead water to us, and now it's given us shelter. It has only meant good things for us, so there must be something good waiting." Heath wasn't so sure. Perhaps it was his natural instinct towards caution, or perhaps it was the pain in his haunch making him cynical. It seemed to him rather more like the stone burrow just existed, Stonecutter Rabbit or not. It didn't seem to have any more motive than rocks or trees. He wondered if in a world where so many things wished death upon the rabbits, perhaps the best they could hope for was neutrality. She must have sensed his disagreement.

"Let me look at the hawk bite," she said, and hopped around him. He lay down, secretly grateful for another rest. He felt her paws and whiskers around his wound, and then her tongue as she started to clean him.

"It's deep," she said, "but it'll heal in time." Heath winced as she found an extra sore spot.

"I didn't ask," she continued, "but why did you slow down in the first place? You could have easily outrun me." Heath sighed. In truth, he didn't have a good answer himself for that question, only that it had seemed like the better odds for both of them to survive.

"I guess it's because I'm a fool," he answered eventually, "but I knew I had a chance against the hawk, and you didn't." His sister considered this in silence for a moment before continuing.

"The Elders wouldn't approve of such things," she said, "but I thank you." She hopped down into the water to get around him, and paused.

"Brother?" she whispered, new fear creeping into her tone.

"What?"

"Which way was the water flowing?" He blinked slowly at

the bizarre question.

"Backwards," he replied. "The way we came."

"Oh," Millet's voice quivered a little. "It's…it's not now." Heath pulled himself to his feet and walked into the water. The current flowed over his paws, stronger than it had been before, and definitely in the opposite direction.

"Why would it do that?" Millet whispered, but he could hear the panic rising in her voice.

"More that I don't know." Heath listened intently down the burrow from which they had come. He could barely make out a very distant rumble, or a growl. He pressed his ear to the stone wall of the burrow. There was definitely a rolling noise coming from behind them. Not the rhythmic beating of a rabbit walking or signalling, but a constant, steady, unsettling noise that he could not identify, but filled him with dread. Somehow he felt going back now was in no way an option.

"What's coming?" Millet asked. He heard her breathing faster and smelled her panic.

"I think," Heath hesitated. *No,* he thought, *this is no time for thinking.* "I think we should be running." Millet didn't need any further encouragement and bolted deeper into the burrow. Heath moved slower and though he could clearly hear her up ahead, his vision in the darkness was useless. There was no light at all to see by now. He couldn't be sure of his footing, but the stone walls of the burrow were regular and predictable so he did not trip. His wound had throbbed with a dull ache while resting, but now the searing pain returned with the increased activity. He dared not stop running. Even the thinking part of his brain did not want to find what was making the noise behind them. He held up his hind leg and ran on three to keep up speed. Suddenly he slipped on the sloped walls and tumbled down into the water at the bottom.

The water level was higher, he realised. Standing on all fours it was already up to his chest and flowing stronger.

He staggered up the other side of the burrow, forced himself to use both hind legs for balance and tried to keep running. Only a few lengths later his soaking wet feet slipped again on the cold stone. He tumbled back into the water, higher already, with small pieces of stick and ash floating in it now. He scrambled to grab the bottom of the burrow with his claws, but could barely reach. The current carried him deeper into the darkness. Heath desperately tried to pull himself to the side, but the churning water pushed him around and made it difficult to orientate himself. He spluttered as his head ducked under the filthy water. He kicked out and tried to keep himself afloat.

"Run!" he called out, to wherever Millet might be. He still couldn't see her, and all he could hear now was the swirling water in his ears.

It was fear clouding his mind now. The hawk had been bad, but he could see the hawk. He could understand it, he knew what the hawk wanted. The fire was worse, it had no motive, no intention other than to consume, but at least he could still see it, could still perceive an escape route.

The flowing water and the stone burrow was different. He couldn't see it, it had no motive, and the only possible escape was to keep running. But he had already failed to run, and was swept up in the current, dragged deeper into the unknown.

Desperately he tied to stay afloat, to keep precious air in his lungs.

"Brother!" He heard Millet's muffled cry, but he could no longer tell from which direction it came.

He tried to pick a single direction to swim in, tried to find an edge. Every time his claws scrambled at the smooth stone he failed to grab hold, only to be knocked about and disorientated once more. A clump of mud, ash and roots struck his head, and for a moment he sunk under the surface. His legs touched the bottom, and he kicked up to reach air once more, but his stamina was already drained from the previous chase. He knew his strength would not last.

This is the time for thinking, he thought to himself, *running is useless now*. His thoughts were oddly calm, but he felt there was truth there. Running had got him this far, but his body was exhausted. It was up to his brain.

He took a gulp of air and arched his back. His body sank, but his head remained above the water. He spun in the current, knocked against more debris, but kept his nose above the waterline. Other things were in the water now. They bumped against him and spun him round. He had no idea what direction anything was moving in, only that air was up. The roar of the torrent echoed, magnifying itself to a chaotic, deafening, clamour, making it near impossible to hear his surroundings.

The debris floats, he thought, *that would be helpful*. A hard, rough object collided with him. He scraped his claws over it, desperate for a foothold. Flecks of bark dislodged between his toes, almost holding, but then breaking and drifting away.

Heath washed up briefly on the sloped stone wall, stole a few breaths of fresh air and tried to listen around. He had no idea where his sister was, but only a moment to think of her before something struck his haunch and pulled him under the water once more. He kicked and paddled aimlessly, hoping that somehow he would pull himself up again into air.

It felt like forever before his head was above water again, spinning through the noisy dark. He coughed and spluttered, dislodging the ash-laden water from his nose and flailed about trying to right himself.

His front paw connected with something softer, and grassy. His claws dug into its weave and mercifully held. He reached across to grab whatever it was with his other paw. It held. He realised it was some sort of matted dry grass, light enough to float. Hoping, he pulled his chest up onto it. The grass sank a little under his weight, but kept his front half above the surface, hind legs dragging in the turbulent water. He clung on for dear life, lying as flat as possible, still spinning in the current. Filthy water poured from his ears and drenched fur. Even now, the grass smelled like home, comforting somehow. The familiar scent coupled with exhaustion almost made him drift into sleep.

Something splashed behind him as it fell into the current.

He still could not see a thing, but he heard it continuing to splash and struggle. He realised it might be Millet.

"Grab something!" he yelled. His cry echoed through the burrow, but the noise of the water drowned his sound. The thrashing thing was near him now but he dared not move from his grip on the grass raft. Small claws raked across his injured leg. He shrieked in pain, but the claws didn't catch, they only pushed him away, spinning, in the current. His back bumped into the stone wall behind him. It was steeper than he remembered, almost vertical. He'd have no hope of climbing out of the water now. In a moment of calm thoughts he wondered whether the walls of the burrow had changed, or, more likely, whether the water level had risen.

He thought the splashing had stopped though it was hard to be certain between the noise of the water and his waterlogged ears. He tried to listen, but needed all his energy to simply hold onto the grass raft. Even with the raft, his head would almost fall under the water, and small waves frequently washed over him,

Suddenly a beam of light pierced the darkness ahead. A narrow hole in the roof of the burrow, big enough to squeeze through but so far out of reach. For a moment he saw what lay ahead of him. Churning water, mud and ash had swept with it chunks of debris, partially burnt grass, sticks and logs. The torrent carried clumps of dried earth around him, he saw them crumbling in the brief of light.

The water had indeed risen to half way up the height of the round stone burrow. There was nothing to grab, nowhere to climb out onto. It would take all his strength to hold on until the water had taken him wherever it was going. He almost wished they had remained in darkness.

And there, ahead of him, was Millet. Half-drowned, like him she clung to debris to keep her head above the water. *A half burned log*, he realised, before the moment of light passed them and they floated deeper into the burrow.

He had no idea how fast the water was flowing, he thought there might have been turns, but he spun around so often he couldn't tell. Another small hole and beam of light approached, though he couldn't be certain that it wasn't the same one.

"Sister?" he called. Her grip lacked strength, her hold tenacious at best. In the brief gap of light he saw her ears lift in response. She tried to pull herself higher onto the log, slipped and fell back. Heath winced. He desperately wanted to help but he could do nothing from his raft. He had no way to reach her. In any case he would not be able to pull her onto his raft of grass, even if it would take both their weights. He couldn't help her this time.

The current pulled them way from the light once more and onward into the stone burrow. *If there is a Great Stonecutter Rabbit,* Heath thought, *he's surely awake now. Is it possible he will help us?*

"I can't hold on!" Millet cried, half choked by the water.

"You must!" Heath replied, "Please hold on, it's our only hope." *I'd be so grateful,* he thought, *to be in the sun again, to feel earth beneath my feet. Please let us escape this.* He wasn't certain who his thoughts were asking, but clinging to the grass raft for his life, all he could do now was hope and think.

Another beam of light waited up ahead. *How many was that,* he wondered. *Are they all different, or the same one, going round in circles? Does this burrow even go anywhere?*

In the dim light he spied his sister, wide-eyed, looking around with desperation and fear. She was slipping on the log. He barely made out long scratches in its scorched bark where she had been trying to hold on. As the water carried them under the light he saw her focus on another branch in the debris, smaller and floating lower in the water. She took a deep breath, braced herself against the log one last time and kicked off with all her might.

The kick lifted her half her height out of the ash-laden water. She spun at the peak of her jump, and reached for the smaller branch, landing half way across it. Both she and the branch sank into the water, and Heath felt as though his heart was beating in his throat. She bobbed to the surface in the middle of the branch before they both floated out of reach of the light.

"I'm okay!" she called out before being muffled by a splash of water. "Mostly!"

"Just hold on," Heath called back, hoping he would take his own advice.

"Where do you think we're going?" she yelled. He didn't reply immediately, tried to grasp a solid answer. He didn't know the world beyond the warren and had only heard tales of other warrens from newcomers like Bracken. As far as he recalled, the entire world consisted of different warrens and their rabbits. Bracken and Flax had told many stories, but none of them gave him any idea of what might lie ahead.

"Let me guess," Millet continued between the bobbing of her branch, "you don't know." He dared to look forward, or what he assumed was forward. At least the water seemed to be taking them in that direction. Perhaps his desperate, hopeful mind was imagining things, but the world seemed brighter ahead.

"We'll find out soon!" he called back. He was shivering, something he'd not done all Summer. A few hours ago being cold had seemed an impossible task of his imagination. Here, clinging to floating debris in tumultuous waters streaming underground in the depths of the stone burrow, it was the heat that he barely remembered.

"Maybe it'll take us home?" Millet called hopefully. Heath doubted this would be so.

"It'll take us wherever we need to be." The light grew as they drifted closer. He dared to hope that whatever might be out there would be kind to them. Perhaps there would be another warren, with friendly rabbits that might welcome them and their story, with a particularly welcoming doe and no hawks in sight.

The thought occurred, however, that this was unlikely. There was probably no Great Stonecutter Rabbit out there. He couldn't be certain of what awaited them, but he knew that they'd find lots of water, and open sky. They would be exposed and wet, and he wouldn't be surprised if they met another hawk. Ah, the hawk. Now that was a creature with a plan.

A flicker of dread rose in his thoughts. Surely the hawk could see very far from high in the sky. Perhaps it knew where the stone burrow went. Perhaps it knew where they would surface.

It might be waiting.

All they could do when they left the burrow would be to seek shelter. They couldn't know which way to run, or where to look. His thinking mind was useless now, faced with the unknown and suspense. All it thought of was a long list of horrible things to go wrong.

He tensed his legs in anticipation. They drifted ever closer to the light, and he almost distinguished details now. More pale grey stone walls, like the entrance at home, and patches of strange colour. Water had flowed out there, numerous objects floated in the slush.

It seemed all too sudden that the water flowed out of the darkness and into the light.

Uncertainty itself was the worst
suffering.

Heath looked around rapidly. Either side of the flowing water
sloped steep grey stone, just like at home, but he saw no

crumbled debris or path to climb up. They were both soaking wet, their paws would be slippery. He knew he would have had a hard enough time climbing those walls when he was fresh. He doubted he'd manage now he was exhausted, drenched and wounded. He scanned the darkening sky. No hawk to be seen.

A small blessing.

The water gushed out of the stone burrow and slowed in the wider channel. Both rabbits scanned their surroundings, near panic. There was nowhere to climb. Mud and debris coated the bottom of the channel, only added to by the ash and plant laden water that carried them now. The water slowed to lap at the silt covered shore at the bottom of the grey stone slopes. They couldn't stay here, soaking wet with no shelter. *Now or never,* he thought. He let himself slip off his grass raft and tried to swim into the shallows. The silt and mud stuck to his feet, and took extra strength to pull himself through it. Millet splashed behind him, but he did not turn to look. He was fairly sure she would keep up, and in any case his injury concerned him more.

Stagnant pools of water dotted the muddy canal, though it did not appear to have rained here recently. Heath wasn't certain how far they might have travelled in the torrent, but it must have outrun both the fire and the storm. The only scent of smoke rose from his own fur, and even that was weak, covered as he had been in water and debris.

He heard Millet working her way through the sludge behind him. She was lighter than him, and not sinking quite so much. He supposed she didn't dare call out while they were exposed to ask him yet another question for which he'd have no answer.

Did our ancestors spend so much time not knowing things? he wondered. *Is life no more than an endless string of questions to navigate?* The Elders never admitted to not knowing. At least the ground he waded through was closer to solid, which had to be an improvement.

His thinking mind nudged its way back into his surface thoughts. He left very deep footprints in the mud as he walked. He paused to consider this more closely. There were definitely no tracks but their own, no scent of anyone else having been down here. No rabbits, no foxes, no footprints of any kind.

Of course, that didn't mean there wouldn't be a hawk around, somewhere. The steep stone banks here were not quite the same as home. Patches of distinct, bright colours covered sections of stone like moss on a log, though they resembled no plant that Heath knew. They appeared to be flat, a part of the stone itself, but garishly coloured like rare windflowers and butterflies. There was no apparent meaning or pattern as far as he could tell, though the colours seemed to follow themselves within the patch. The banks of the stone burrow at home had been stark and bare, the same monotonous grey the whole way around. He wondered what the colours were for, or what they might signify.

Either way, they didn't offer them a way out.

He tried to look beyond the stone banks, to try to understand where they were. Tops of trees were barely visible, far greener than the Eucalypt of home had been. They were too far away for Heath to know much more about them. Among some of the trees he also saw strange angular shapes, equally as tall as the trees themselves, though he couldn't imagine what they might be.

"It's not what I'd hoped for," Millet admitted as she plodded up beside him. She was absolutely dripping wet, her fur stuck flat against her somewhat scrawny body, and he supposed he must be the same.

"Were you hoping for anything other than to be alive?" Millet actually laughed once in reply.

"Some grass would be nice, and solid ground."

"We wouldn't be that lucky." Mosquitoes rose from the shallow, stagnant pools as they approached. Heath looked back at their tracks, just in case anything followed them from the Great Stonecutter Rabbit's burrow. He saw nothing but water and debris. It felt like they'd been walking much further than they actually had. The sky started to dim behind the grey storm clouds as dusk approached. They needed shelter to rest. He simply could not keep going like this, and he doubted his sister was any stronger. Neither of them mustered up the strength to run across the mud, so they continued with a steady, sticky plod. The mud became drier the further they walked, even more so as they veered towards one of the edges.

So this is where our water came from, Heath mused. *Not quite the mystery I imagined it would be.*

Ahead Heath noticed a small bush which had uprooted and fallen down the slope. It lay there on its side, roots exposed, leaves still baring the faintest hint of green. Millet chose to wander towards it, Heath found himself without the strength to pick up speed. Every muscle in his body ached from exertion, and some in his hip from both fatigue and the hawk's wound. She sniffed the leaves cautiously, inspecting them one at a time.

"I think we can eat these," she said, "Though I've never seen them before. Caterpillars have eaten some of the leaves, so it can't be that bad." She started picking the greener leaves from the dried branches and began eating. Heath caught up to her a moment later, stopping to catch his breath.

Millet busied herself with food, and his stomach keenly reminded him that he was hungry too. His thinking mind preoccupied itself with the other half of the bush, pushing his hunger aside. The roots had caught some mud on themselves, and might provide enough support to attempt a shallow burrow. They both needed to rest, but it was so dangerous out in the open. Here at least they had some meager food, and a little shelter. He certainly had found enough water for one day.

Millet dropped a mouthful of leaves in front of him.

"Eat," she urged him, like a mother doe with a forgetful kit, as she turned back to select more leaves. He took a bite, finding the leaves tougher than the grass of the warren, but he knew his sister was right; they both needed to eat.

After a few slow mouthfuls Heath hopped to the roots of the bush and investigated the mud there. After a few tentative scratches Millet joined him.

"What are you doing?" she asked.

"I thought if we dug a shallow burrow of our own, one of us

could sleep while the other stands guard." He scraped some more at the half-dried mud and roots, digging slowly.

"Let me help," his sister offered.

"No," he replied. "You pick more food." Obligingly, Millet went to do so, still keeping a eye on the darkening sky. Heath dug much slower than he usually would have, partly due to caution and partly due to exhaustion. As he dug, Millet piled more selected leaves beside him.

He felt ready to collapse when Millet finally nudged him.

"Please stop. Please eat. I'll keep digging," she offered. Reluctantly Heath took a step back.

"It's almost big enough for you anyway," he sighed. He flopped down next to the food and gratefully began to eat. The taste mattered less now; he barely kept his eyes open. He let Millet dig, piling mud up around the entrance, until she could easily fit in the makeshift burrow.

"You rest there," he told her. "I'll guard the entrance, and then swap when you're rested." She nodded and attempted to curl herself up in the meager shelter the hole provided. Covered in mud from nose to tail, Heath realised she was simply too tired to clean herself. He positioned himself in the entrance, looking out over the mud and stone banks, listening intently while he ate the unappetising leaves. Muffled, soft noises drifted down from the banks above, but he saw no sign of movement. The only noise nearby was the swarm of mosquitoes, which had risen from the many stagnant pools behind them. They fed from his ears and wound, seeking his warm skin between the cracks of the drying mud. He didn't have the energy to try to drive them away, so just let them feed.

He sat perfectly still, scanning the dusk sky and the stone banks. Tomorrow they would have to try to find a way out. He supposed it might be possible to go back through the stone burrow, if the water cleared. If it was still flooded they would have no hope of swimming in their weakened state. Also, trying to remember, he couldn't be certain there hadn't been forks in the path. It had all been too disorientating to keep track of where they were going at the time. How many days would it take them to swim the burrow? Far too long.

The only option was to try to get up the stone banks. Hopefully there would be some decent grass and a chance to properly recuperate before attempting an overland journey home. But which direction to go? He assumed the stone burrow travelled more or less straight, but the more he thought about it the less certain he became. They might end up in a completely different direction. They may never see the warren again.

This idea was not as distressing as he expected it to be. He was a young buck, and would have been expected to move on from the warren eventually anyway. The day would have come when he turned his back on the warren, never returning, seeking a burrow and a doe for his own. Now here he stood, far from his home. He even had a doe, but while there was technically nothing wrong with Millet she wasn't quite the type of doe he'd had in mind.

She slept quietly behind him now. He wondered what she thought about it all. If she hadn't been so thirsty today, would they have ended up on the other side of the fire? Would they be safe in their warren under the Eucalypt tonight, or would they be burned and eaten?

Some rabbits of the warren had developed the idea that everything around them was placed there with purpose, just for them, by some kind spirit that came before them. His older cousin Lantana had been a particularly firm advocate of this way of thinking. He often overheard her explaining it to her kits. She claimed that the kind spirit was the reason the stone burrow existed, why the Eucalypt was so strong and the grass so good. Heath wasn't so sure. Yes, there were good things in their world, but there were bad things too, like all the creatures that wished them death. He remembered asking her what put the predators, bringers of death and pain, into the world for the rabbits. Well, obviously not the kind spirit, she had replied, and hurried to take her kits elsewhere, avoiding any further questions. She had not been happy with his questioning. It seemed Lantana and rabbits like her liked their own thoughts, the comforting ones, but not the difficult questions. Which was more likely to keep a rabbit alive: comforting thoughts, or difficult questions?

Well, he thought, *we're still alive now. There's plenty of difficult questions, but not so much comforting thoughts.*

His un-rabbit-like thoughts froze for a moment. Something scampered on the stone ledge. The movement was brief and erratic, but it was there. Heath dared not move, not knowing what lurked above him. Barely anything was visible over the tops of the stone banks, but he thought there was a subtle twinkle of small, bright eyes. He blinked, and a moment later the small eyes vanished. He couldn't be sure whether he had been seen, but suddenly felt more uneasy knowing there were creatures up there, than when he believed they were alone.

Heath could see relatively well in the moon and starlight, and now watched the stone banks with extra caution. He couldn't hear the creatures up there. *Maybe,* he thought, *they're watching me as closely as I'm watching them.*

He couldn't decide whether or not that was a bad thing. If they feared him, then they'd be less likely to try and eat him, but alternatively they might know a way up the stone banks. He dared not move yet. He and his sister had done so much this day that the opportunity to rest was vital. The surveillance stalemate could continue until they were both rested. Actually, he wasn't even sure that they knew Millet was here, obscured in their muddy hole. He decided to just look and listen until she was rested and they were as dry as possible before attempting to climb the stone banks.

The mosquitoes left him as the night cooled. The heat of Summer was still present, so it wasn't unbearably cold, even in the open. He wondered what little creatures might be waiting up there. They clearly had more sense than to come down here, into the mud.

It was so quiet. After the roaring water of the stone burrow his ears rang in the silence. All he could do now was observe, listen and think. He doubted there was a Great Stonecutter Rabbit any more. *After all, shouldn't there be footprints?*

The stars above were the same as the ones at home. *The clouds always change,* he thought, *but the stars are the same. I suppose that's one small comfort, at least.*

He barely noticed the movement above the stone ledge and flattened himself in fright. Something squeaked, but it was quickly silenced. A moment later, a pale shape appeared and flew over the stone bank. It dipped towards him before flapping and gaining height. The pale underside of its wings seemed to glow in the moonlight. Powerful talons, not unlike the hawk, clutched something small and unfortunate, trailing a skink-like tail. Heath watched it fly over to the other stone bank, gaining height, and disappeared. He hadn't heard it make a sound.

Heath suddenly felt a lot less safe. *Still,* he thought, *at least it's not eating me.*

Yet.

He considered his options. They had nowhere better to run to, nowhere better to hide. They could try to climb the stone banks, but he knew some kind of creature was up there. No, much better to wait.

Several hours passed. On occasion Heath thought he saw more small eyes peering over the bank, but only for a moment or two each time. Nothing approached them, nothing else flew overhead. Eventually Millet stirred from her sleep and pushed her way out from behind him. The moon was high in the sky now.

"You need to rest too," she reminded him. He stretched and shuffled his way into the muddy burrow, slightly too small for him.

"There are creatures up there," he whispered, "But they've not tried to come down here." She squatted at the entrance, listening intently.

"I'll watch for them," she replied softly, "Now you have to rest. You have to rest to run tomorrow."

Heath fell into a dreamless sleep faster than he expected. He felt like he only blinked before the dark night sky was replaced with the pale glow of approaching dawn. For a moment he couldn't remember where he was, but then the memories of yesterday came rushing back. The heat, the fire, the hawk and the water. It was probably a mercy that he hadn't dreamed. His sister was alert, staring at the near bank. He nudged her from behind. She took a small hop forward, still staring at the bank. He followed her gaze; there was definitely movement up there.

"They keep coming to look," she told him. "Sometimes they make a little noise before running away. I think they're curious." He watched the creatures atop the stone banks patiently, listening around them all the while.

As Millet had said, one of them stepped forward, leaning a little over the edge to stare down at them. Those were the tiny twinkling eyes he had seen. They belonged to a small brown creature with a pointed nose and tiny ears. It squeaked at them and seemed to be waiting for a response.

"Hello!" Millet cried out to it before Heath could stop her.

"What was that for?" he hissed at her, scanning the horizon.

"Huh?"

"There are hunters here!" he hissed. "Silent flyers, like hawks in the night! They'll hear you!" Heath nervously scanned the sky. There was no point in thumping his foot against the ground in warning, they were the only two rabbits here.

"You didn't tell me!" Millet hissed back, catching his fear. The small creature on the bank squeaked again.

"Don't reply," Heath said, stepping between Millet and the stone bank, "You'll attract a hunter." Millet's eyes widened. She too scanned the surroundings, but there was no immediate threat. Heath looked around. They'd have to run, further up the canal. It would be their only choice.

"They must know that too," Millet said. "If they're risking attention, maybe they want to help us?" Heath was dubious. What would these tiny creatures have to gain by helping them? The small creature disappeared from sight. The rabbits waited a moment to see whether they would reappear.

"I think we should go," Heath said, "as far as we can manage. Hopefully there will be something we can climb." He turned and hopped slowly through the silt, waiting for his sister to follow. She didn't. Instead she hopped toward the bank.

"What are you doing?" he demanded.

"I really think they want to help," she said firmly. "I'm going to try to climb up there."

"You could barely climb the rubble back home," he scoffed. "What makes you think you can climb the intact stone? We should go." Millet ignored him and tried to scramble up the smooth slope. Her muddy paws did not grip the smooth surface well. She managed only a few paces before skidding down.

"I told you," Heath stated. She stubbornly ignored him again. This time she tried running up the slope at full speed before slipping and tumbling back down in a heap. She lay there panting for a moment. Heath hopped back to her. At the top of the stone slope, three small, brown, pointed faces stared down at them.

"You're not strong enough" he said softly, "and neither am I right now. Let's go." Millet didn't move to get up and crossly ignored him. He sat down beside her, gazing down the muddy canal where he hoped they would find a way up the banks.

"I won't go without you, you know."

"I know," she admitted, "But I want to know what they are. I don't think they mean to hurt us."

"They want to know what you eat," a small voice called from above. The rabbits looked up to the row of small faces. They had been joined by a larger face of similar shape. This larger creature was easily ten times the size of the small ones though still much smaller than either of the rabbits. Its long nose was tipped with elegant whiskers and while mostly brown like its smaller companions, had a white blaze of fur running asymmetrically between its eyes.

"Who are you?" Heath called up, suspicious of the strangers and wary of the attention they were doubtlessly generating. The creature sat up on the edge of the stone bank. It has short legs ending in nimble fingers.

"I am Stares-at-moon," it said with an air of pride. It reached behind itself to pick up its tail. It was long and almost hairless, not unlike a skink tail. Heath wondered whether the silent flyer had captured one of its kin last night.

"I am a long tail," it continued. "I speak for the small folk. They do not speak themselves, you see, though if you are very fortunate indeed, you may yet hear them sing." It regarded the two rabbits over the end of its long nose.

"However, from where I stand now, you do not appear to be the fortunate type." Millet pulled herself to her feet and sat up as tall as possible.

"We eat grass and flowers and leaves," she said, as loudly as she dared. "We eat plants that grow, not creatures that run. Please, can you help us?"

"Hear that boys?" said Stares-at-moon. "The fluffy-butts here eat grass and flowers and leaves. Not your squeaky selves. What do you make of that, eh?" The three small folk, as Stares-at-moon had called them, disappeared from the rabbits view.

"Well now that is a thing," the long tail mused to itself. "And what might you fluffy-butts be doing here? That's an unfortunate place to be if ever I saw one. Not a blade of grass down there for you."

"The sky above our warren struck the trees, setting the world aflame. We were chased by a hawk into the stone burrow, and then washed here with the water," said Heath. He hopped right up to the bank and placed one foot upon it. "We were running for our lives. Will you help us get out?"

"Well now, we shall have to see," replied Stares-at-moon. "There's no telling what the small folk might do until they go and do it. But I'll tell you what, just sit tight, and I'll see if I can know their mind." The long tail vanished from sight.

We were ordinary street rats.

"I told you they'd help us," Millet said. In spite of the mud and filth, she seemed somewhat happier. Heath shook his head and hopped back to the scant shelter of the bush. They had already made a lot of noise and he didn't like the odds of a predator being attracted by it.

The sun rose slowly. Soon the summer heat would follow. He decided there was no point being out in the open, so he lay down in the tiny scrap of shade afforded by the bush. Millet remained where she was, listening intently and watching for the creatures' return. Or danger.

There were other creatures around the warren that talked

though they rarely spoke to rabbits. He had seen skinks meeting and appearing to converse, but never with him. They would always scatter and flee if he ever attempted to get close to them. The birds sang, and sometimes the magpies would curse; but aside from the hawk, none had spoken to him before. Then, of course, there was the local wombat. He certainly looked at you like he understood, but never said a word and would walk over you like he didn't care. Heath would never have thought to ask him for help. He never would have dared.

Millet thumped twice on the ground to alert him to movement. At the top of the stone bank one of the small folk had appeared. It squeaked at Millet, then dropped a dandelion flower over the edge.

Heath sat up, suddenly interested. They might help after all. Millet stretched up, but the flower was too far out of reach on the ledge.

"Can you throw it further?" she asked. It reached for the flower, but its little arms were far too short. Millet sat back down.

"Well, thank you for trying," she said, though Heath heard the disappointment in her voice. The small folk vanished back over the ledge.

"Well, we gave it a chance," said Heath. "If we wait too long it will get too hot to travel."

"I just…" Millet sighed and hopped back towards him, "I hoped it would be a way, somehow…" she paused, ears twitching, and spun back to face the stone bank. Two of the small folk appeared at the ledge. Between them, they were dragging a twig. The rabbits stared as they manoeuvred the twig carefully down the ledge to nudge the dandelion flower further down the stone. With considerable care and dexterity they flicked the dandelion further down the slope. Millet backed up for a running start, bounded a few paces up the ledge and barely managed to grab the flower. She slid down and looked up at the small folk, dandelion between her teeth. They were watching her expectantly.

"Thank you!" she called up to them and leapt a little with joy. She picked up the dandelion once more and skipped back to her brother.

"Do you want half?" she offered. He shook his head but his stomach rumbled.

"No," he said, walking past her. "I want out." He hopped up to the stone banks where the small folk were staring. The dandelion was understandably large in their tiny hands, but it would be insignificant in the rabbits' stomachs.

"Stares-at-moon!" Heath shouted, no longer caring about predators. "Stares-at-moon! Are you there?" There was no immediate response. He thumped his uninjured leg impatiently, the noise echoed off the stone banks. The small folk scattered at the noise with a chorus of tiny squeaks.

"Oh, for creatures that like to hide you are a noisy pair," said the long tail, peering over the edge. "What is it, fluffy-butt?"

"Listen," said Heath urgently, "Can your small folk find a bigger stick? Something we can reach and climb?" Stares-at-moon cocked its head to one side.

"That's a very big ask for some very small folk," it remarked.

"Yes I suppose it is," Heath admitted, "But I think it's our only chance. One dandelion flower isn't enough of a meal for either of us. Unless you can tell me of an easier path up the stone slopes somewhere else, we'll be stuck here. We will starve without your help." Stares-at-moon combed its whiskers with its nimble fingers in contemplation.

"No," it replied after contemplation. "These banks are steep for all the distance I know. There is no easier path up."

"So what do you do if someone falls in?" Millet asked.

"I'm afraid the ghosts in the night take them," it replied. Heath remembered the silent flyer from the previous night. It hadn't paid them any attention, but that didn't mean it wouldn't do so tonight. After all, last night it already had a meal in its talons.

"So," Millet wondered, looking behind her at the opposite bank. "Do any of you ever go to the other side?" *I wouldn't think so*, thought Heath, *that's where the night flyer went.*

"There is a path to cross from one side to the other," said Stares-at-moon, gesturing further down the canal. "Over the top, but we rarely cross it. It's far away, and we have little need to do so. We call it the Over Path."

Heath turned to his sister. "I think we should go find it," he said. "We can't climb up here and there's little shelter. If they won't help us we need to look for something else. But I won't leave you here."

"Oh, I never said they wouldn't help," the long tail called down to them as it turned to leave, "Just that I'm not sure they can. You're a thousand times bigger than they are. How will one more twig help you? You need the whole tree!"

Stares-at-moon scampered out of sight, leaving the two

rabbits in relative silence.

They waited for a moment, in case anyone returned.

"Let's find the Over Path," Heath decided. "If nothing else it might bring some shade when the heat comes."

"Okay," Millet begrudgingly agreed. They travelled further down the canal, the mud at the bottom was beginning to dry, but still retained too much moisture to be easy travelling. Heath often lagged behind and his sister would patiently wait for him to catch up, scanning the surrounds for predators. The hawk's wound was more trouble than he thought it would be, but he didn't regret his recklessness. Not while his sister hopped beside him.

The sun was high in the sky when Millet finally stopped. "Do you think that's it?" she wondered, sitting as tall as she could manage for a better view. Heath looked up. He hadn't been watching where they were going. It had been too much physical effort to keep his head up and eyes forward. Instead he simply followed his sister, trusting that she would notice anything important, while he focused on where he placed his feet. He stopped to look now.

At the top of the stone banks, spanning the gap, was more stone. It arched easily over the banks, but still so far out of reach. There were regular smooth grey columns reaching up to the sky along either edge of it. Thick ivy and tufts of long grass had grown over some of the columns.

Oh, how he wanted the grass. *Up there must be paradise compared to down here,* he thought.

Where the path met the bank a small amount of ivy had grown a few paces into the canal. It was too high for a rabbit to reach, but it stirred Heath's thinking mind. An idea began to form.

"If only that ivy grew down here," he said. "Then we might be able to climb up."

"Maybe it will be on the other side?" Millet hoped. She took off at a sprint to bound under the pathway and out the other side. Heath took some time to catch up to her at his slower pace.

"There's not," she said sadly, hopping back into shade, "but it was a good thought." Heath stood up as tall as he dared and looked around, wincing a little at the pain in his hip. The canal ahead looked almost identical to the canal behind. The only noticeable difference was the pair of rabbit footprints in the mud from where they had come, and he scolded himself for leaving such an obvious trail.

No, he thought, *we need to hold onto this idea. Don't lose focus. It might work, we just need a little help.*

He hopped back the way they had come.

"Stares-at-moon!" Heath called, thumping his feet. The noise echoed subtly off the stone banks. "We need you! Stares-at-moon!" He waited in the open, earnestly hoping that the long tail and the small folk would appear.

"Maybe they can't hear us?" Millet suggested. "I'm sure they have their own things to do." Heath wandered back into the shade, listening for movement all the while. He flopped down in the shadow of the Over Path, grateful for the little shelter it would give. He hated being injured and the weakness it caused him.

"What do we do now?" Millet crept close and whispered to

him. He lay down on his side, shut his eyes and sighed.

"Wait. I need to rest some more." He wanted badly for his idea to work. The true rabbit thoughts, the sort the Elders approved of, had no better plan to just keep going until they either found a way to climb out, or died. They would never approve of asking the small folk for help. They would not have approved of a fast rabbit slowing down to divert the attack of a hawk either.

But the Elders weren't here now to govern his thoughts or reprimand his ideas. They were alone out here, without their rules and guidance. Perhaps it was time for new thoughts.

Millet sat beside him, vigilant for danger. She took the opportunity to clean some of the mud from her fur.

"You know," she said after she had cleaned her paws, "I never imagined I would travel far from the warren. I thought I'd line a burrow and have kits. This is unimaginable."

"Nobody would have thought of this," Heath replied, his eyes half closed. "I assumed beyond the warren were more warrens. Looks like sometimes the world is different."

"Is different good or bad?"

"Neither. It just is."

Having cleaned her paws, Millet began to clean her exhausted brother's face. She nibbled off the dried mud and rubbed his ears clean. When that was done, she looked at his wound once more. She fussed over the injury in silence.

"How does it look?" he asked when she said nothing.

"It would be fine if you actually rested and hadn't been caught up in this…this adventure," she half scolded him.

"Would you rather I hadn't?" he asked, opening one eye to

watch her reaction. She sighed.

"No," she admitted, "I'm thankful you came with me to lookout while I drank, and everything since." New thoughts jostled for a position in Heath's mind. He hadn't considered the possibility that the strife they were in now could be blamed on Millet. If she hadn't needed that water so badly, if he hadn't gone with her, they likely wouldn't be here now. At least, he wouldn't be.

He banished the thought from his mind. Of course it wasn't her fault. She couldn't help becoming thirsty. His sister didn't start the fire and she didn't summon the hawk. She certainly didn't make it rain and flood the burrow. What cruel thoughts they were, to blame someone for events beyond their control.

Those thoughts were simply not welcome in his head.

"Hoi, fluffy-butts!" called a familiar voice. "You were hollering?" The rabbits scampered out from under the Over Path. There, cleaning its whiskers on the edge of steep stone bank next to the ivy, was Stares-at-moon.

"That is not a clever thing for a clever creature to do," it said merrily. "Unless perhaps you wanted the ghosts in the night to pick you up and carry your bodies away? That's one way to get out of the mud!"

"I know it's not wise, but we need help," said Heath, "and you and your folk are the only ones we know. I understand I asked too much before to bring us something to climb, but please listen to me, I have a new idea."

The long tail's whiskers twitched in curiosity. "A clever long tail always listens, perchance to learn," it said, leaning closer to listen. "Do go on." Heath stepped forward and gestured to the ivy growing up the protrusions along the Over Path.

"Well, I'm pretty sure anyway, that we would be able to climb that ivy if it was growing on these slopes," he began. "It's already here, and anchored on the ground where you are now, just too high."

"Go on," said Stares-at-moon, folding its fingertips in front of its face.

"Well, if the small folk could be so good, so nimble, as to climb into the ivy and chew its bonds from the path, it should fall down. Then we can climb up."

"I see," mused the long tail, "and what do you propose to do then, once you are up here with us?"

"We will try to go home," Heath replied. Stares-at-moon peered down its long nose at the two rabbits.

"That's all?" it asked, somewhat incredulously. "All you can offer is to leave? Surely there must be more to you than just running away?"

Heath was taken aback, he was sure his idea had been a good one. He hadn't considered why the small folk wouldn't have simply gone along with it.

"We can dig," Millet spoke up, joining her brother in their plea. "We can dig vast burrows to shelter in. And we're much bigger than you. We could carry things. We're very fast," she paused, glancing at her brother's wound. "Usually. What can we do to be of service to you?"

"Hmm," Stares-at-moon considered. "I shall tell the small folk this. However be aware, I am not their master in any way. I simply offer them words they do not have."

"If there is nothing we can offer them," Millet continued, "please thank them. They would have our gratitude."

"And what is gratitude worth, to the small folk or to a fluffy-butt?" asked Stares-at-moon, though Heath wasn't sure that the long tail truly expected an answer.

"Everything," Millet said softly. "Absolutely everything." The long tail chuckled a little, took a bow, and vanished back over the bank.

"Do you think they'll help?" Millet asked her brother. Heath turned away from the ledge and shuffled back to the shade.

"Maybe," he replied, "I hope so." Millet followed him back into the shade of the Over Path. Heath investigated the dirt closest to the banks. It seemed much drier here, more sandy. He started digging slowly, concluding that if they were going to wait for the small folk, they might as well try to be comfortable.

"I wish we had more food," Millet pined, hunched and looking worried. "My tummy is so empty." Heath sniffed the shallow hole he had made. It was barely a few paws deep, and already he had encountered the impenetrable grey stone of the banks and burrow.

"We can't dig any further here," he said. "There's more stone underneath." Millet hopped over to investigate.

"It must go all the way down," she mused. "Now what do we do?"

"Wait," Heath suggested, flopping down in the shade beside the bank, "Wait and see if they want to help us. Otherwise you go on as far as you can without me and look for a way up. We both know I'm slowing you down." Millet watched him in silence. Heath sensed she wanted to disagree, but knew he had a point. He realised however that just because she was silent, didn't mean she'd comply. They waited in silence for a time, hunger making them more tired than usual. Heath preoccupied himself by examining their surroundings. The grey stone was splattered with coloured patches here too. Some colours were simple streaks in one shade, others clearly more elaborate patterns in multiple hues. They were more vivid under the Over Path where the sun didn't reach them. They were a brilliant contrast against the bleak grey even in the bright light. There was clearly some sort of reason or purpose to them, though Heath couldn't decipher what it was. He had to wonder why there were no colours like these on the grey stone near the burrow.

"Do you think they'll believe us when we get home?" Millet asked. *What a strange thought,* Heath mused, *to assume we will actually get there.* They hadn't even managed to climb up the stone banks yet. Every step they had taken was further away from the warren and the Great Eucalypt. *How could she even assume that we would ever get back home?*

"I don't know," he chose to say instead. "Try to rest while we wait."

The sun was sinking low in the sky when Heath heard movement on the path above. He listened carefully and sniffed the breeze. There was no scent of any predator he was familiar with. Listening was hampered a little by the cumbersome summer blowflies that had found the rabbits even here. Now that was one type of creature Heath was grateful that didn't speak.

Gingerly, he rose to his feet and shook the flies away. Millet stood up on her haunches, ears up, straining to listen. Neither spoke.

There was a strange noise; a high-pitched, almost cricket-like vibration. The sound rose and fell in slow waves, unlike anything the rabbits had heard before. Millet exchanged a glance with her brother. Both were wide-eyed, hearts pounding, but she crept out from under the Over Path anyway.

"What are you doing?" he whispered urgently. "We should stay hidden."

"I just want to see," she whispered back. "It's beautiful." Heath blinked slowly. He understood many things were beautiful; the fresh green grass, healthy wide-eyed kits and fresh water, but he had never heard a sound described that way. He realised she wasn't wrong, though he didn't understand why. He followed her out and stared up at the ivy. On the edge of the stone bank sat Stares-at-moon, bobbing its head and swaying its little arms in time with the waves of sound. Dozens of twinkling eyes of the small folk peeked through the ivy, shimmering away.

Stares-at-moon glanced down at the rabbits and waved briefly without saying a word, before going back to the rhythmic swaying. Health wondered if he was swaying in time with the sound unintentionally.

"Do you think they're helping?" Millet whispered. Heath didn't answer. Not only did he not know, but words felt so strange and out of place amongst the melody.

He tapped his toes in time with the rhythm of the sound,

unconsciously at first. He was surprised at himself, but found the beat fit so well he began thumping his good foot with greater volume. The tapping kept in time with the melody and Stares-at-moon's swaying.

Three progressively rising notes swelled from somewhere within the ivy. It was answered by three descending notes from elsewhere within the plant. The whole patch of ivy was trembling now with the movement of the small folk. Millet joined the rhythmic thumping in time with Heath. It was a strange sensation, feeling the melody vibrate through his body. It was unsettling, but also peaceful. Someone in the ivy sang the three rising notes again, and once more it was answered by the three descending ones.

The sound meant something, somehow. It lacked words but Heath felt meaning was hidden in it somewhere. His proper rabbit thoughts couldn't make any sense of it, and his un-rabbit-like thoughts weren't much better. They knew there was more to the sound, but couldn't grasp the meaning. He wondered if there was a third type of thoughts that he didn't have, that the small folk used.

The melody stopped unexpectedly. The rabbits were caught out and continued to thump for a few beats on their own. They froze, ears erect staring at the ivy.

"Ah, any moment now," Stares-at-moon informed them, "Any moment…"

The ivy on the Over Path slipped and peeled away from the structure beneath it. Heath barely saw the small brown bodies of the small folk scampering away or clinging to the upright grey columns. The ivy fell from the path like a sheet, sliding down itself towards the anxiously waiting rabbits.

They passed down all the roads long ago.

The ivy fell with a rustle, sliding most of the way down the stone bank towards the anxiously waiting rabbits. Above them, on the Over Path, dozens of small folk twitched their noses in unison and scampered away in a wave of fur and tails.

"Well now, fluffy-butts," said Stares-at-moon, firmly prodding the ivy, "here are your vines to freedom. Climb them if you shall."

Millet tentatively took a step onto the slope, paused and looked back at her brother.

"You go first," he urged her. "You're lighter." A look of suspicion fleeted across her face, Heath barely noticed it, before she nodded silently and backed up for a running start. She took a deep breath and sprinted for the ivy, leaping from the base of the canal. Heath watched with bated breath as she sailed through the air and landed heavily, claws scrambling for grip in the dried vine. It stretched under her weight.

It held.

Millet scampered up the ivy, dislodging dried leaves as she ran. Steadily she gained ground until Heath saw her shining white tail vanish over the top of the stone banks. He waited anxiously. Stares-at-moon applauded.

"Good show fluffy-butt! Now one more!" Millet's head appeared over the stone bank.

"I did it!" she squeaked. "There's food up here! Come on!" Relief that his plan worked was quickly replaced by concern for his strength. He'd only have one opportunity to jump.

Heath backed up a little and stretched his hind legs. Resting had helped, but the wound on his hip was stiff and he didn't think he would manage two attempts. If he didn't make it Millet would have to go on alone, and somehow he doubted she would.

He took a deep breath, tensed his muscles, and ran.

Movement that had once felt so good now felt so painful as

his leap landed him amongst the ivy. He landed heavily, the impact sending a pang of pain up his back. The ivy pulled tight beneath him. His claws gripped the loosely interwoven tendrils and stopped him sliding back.

Heath couldn't sprint as his sister had done, simply couldn't bring himself to do it. He sat in the midst of the ivy for a breath, then slowly began to climb. Placing each foot carefully, gripping the dried vines with care he shifted his weight and took a step. He thought some of them would break under his weight, but whether it was through luck or caution, he made it to the top of the stony banks.

Millet was right, there was food here. The surrounding ground was covered in grass, greener than the dried plants around the warren, and scattered with shade from many types of trees. The trees were smaller than the Eucalypt of home, but seemed greener and lusher. Beyond them was a broad pathway of the same grey stone of the banks he had climbed. Beyond that was a wide streak of black stone, cracked in places where more grass had colonised it, then more patches of grass between the common grey stone. Dotted along the black stone sat mounds of rusty objects held slightly off the ground by thick black segments. They looked to Heath like hunched, lumbering creatures covered in plates, but they did not move at all. He stared at them to make sure they posed no threat, but they seemed to be as stationary as stones. In any case they were all confined to the black ground, none encroached onto the grass.

"What is this place?" he asked. The shapes he had seen mixed with the tree tops appeared to be mounds or hills. At a distance they didn't seem to be made of plants, and their regular placing made him uneasy. They had straight, regular edges unlike anything that occurred around the warren, and they seemed eerily tall. They might have even been taller than the Eucalypt of the warren. Around him small folk scurried away into the grass, with only the occasional one glancing back towards him.

"This is our home, fluffy-butt," said Stares-at-moon, waving its little hands about to indicate all Heath could see. "What other answer were you expecting? What other answer is there?"

Heath looked at the long tail closely for the first time. Its fur was a greyish colour overall, not unlike Heath's own, but the fur sat sleeker on its stumpy body. It lacked the powerful legs Heath had for running, but had fine, nimble fingers that never quite stopped fidgeting, even though it was sitting still. The tail was indeed long, and almost hairless. It would be completely useless for signaling danger. The white streak between its eyes curved to the left, creating the shape of a crescent moon and involved one eye, which was red. Heath hadn't noticed the odd coloured eyes from the bottom of the bank and wondered if all long tails were like that. He found it oddly disconcerting though he couldn't explain why and dared not ask about it.

Stares-at-moon looked Heath up and down in return. *I wonder what he thinks of us*, thought Heath.

Millet was already feeding on the grass nearby. Three small folk clustered around her, staring silently. Heath couldn't see where the others had gone. No doubt they had sought out their usual shelters. She paused to look up at him with a mouthful of food. She chewed and swallowed quickly.

"You made it!" she exclaimed. Panting with effort, he hopped across and began to feed beside her. It was the best grass he had ever tasted. Part of him suspected any grass was the best grass when you are starving, but he didn't care. The rabbits ate greedily under the interested gaze of the long tail.

"I haven't seen a creature like you," Heath admitted between mouthfuls.

"I've not seen fluffy-butts like you either," the long tail agreed, combing its whiskers with its long fingers. "Isn't that an interesting thing?"

"I haven't spoken with a creature who wasn't a rabbit," Heath continued. "Are there other creatures here that speak?"

"Whether or not they can speak is a different matter entirely from whether they would speak to you," the long tail said coyly. "You must be worth speaking to." Heath considered the strangeness of their surroundings. The grass was good, but boxed in by regular widths of grey stone. It wasn't like the open plains of grass at home. This wasn't a place for rabbits like him.

"Why don't the small folk speak?" Millet asked, between chewing. Stares-at-moon shrugged and began cleaning the inside of its ears.

"Good question but perhaps the better one is why do any of us speak?" Heath paused and sat up on his haunches as though the extra height might let him see the question more clearly. It was strange to consider the possibility of them not speaking. Rabbits had always talked, hadn't they? It was just the way things were. He stared at the long tail in silence, grass half hanging from his mouth as he completely forgot to chew while navigating the difficult thoughts.

"Is there an answer?" asked Millet, her voice snapping Heath out of his confused thoughts.

A much simpler question, he thought, *or is it?*

"Is there ever an answer?" the long tail wondered in return, "There only ever seems to be more questions. I've met long tails that do not speak though we would seem the same in every other way. I wonder why they would not speak a word, or seem to understand me, yet here I am having a leisurely conversation with you fluffy-butts." Stares-at-moon rose on its hind legs, still much shorter than Heath, and turned its head to regard the rabbit with its red eye.

"Tell me why," the long tail demanded. "Why do you speak, yet many of my kin do not?"

Heath backed away a step and crouched, intimidated by the small creature's intense red glare.

"I don't know," he stammered. "I really don't."

"We've always spoken," Millet insisted, stepping forward. "We've told stories to each other for generations, since the dust fell a long time ago." The long tail lowered itself back to the ground.

"I have heard tales of dust," it said, "and of other creatures that speak of it. Tell me, fluffy-butt, what do your stories tell you of dust?"

"Our Elders tell of their Elders speaking of the evening the dust fell," Millet explained, sitting on her haunches while the long tail listened intently. "They said the sky danced with more colours than dusk, with more colours than held by an eye, and their hearts were afraid. The world was silent as the dust fell from the sky, coating the land with its silent colour. Then sound returned to the world and stories were told."

"I see," said Stares-at-moon, stroking its long chin and twirling its whiskers absentmindedly, "and what happened after that?"

"Why, then we went on being rabbits," Millet replied, blinking in confusion. "Eventually we were born and then there was the fire and the water and now here we are."

"I see," said the long tail now combing through the fur on its belly, "And what happened before the dust? What happened in the days before?" Heath and Millet exchanged a glance. This was a question they had never asked before. They had never considered a story before the dust fell. It was the start of all things. Nobody talked about times before.

Nobody had asked.

"There are no stories of days before the dust," Heath said hesitantly, disturbed by the question. *I wonder why nobody has thought about before the dust,* he wondered to himself.

"Oh come now, there must be!" the long tail insisted, scampering between them. "Your mother must have had her mother, and her mother before her. A long line of mothers going back in time forever. Surely you fluffy-butts didn't just pop out of the ground fully formed! It follows that there must have been more of your kind before you. If there were already fluffy-butts there to marvel at the falling dust, there must have been others before. So tell me, what do you know of the days before the dust?" Heath looked at his worried sister. He knew she had no answer for the inquisitive creature, and in truth neither did he.

"I suppose our kind didn't tell stories then," he said, hoping that would be the end of the conversation. It was the only answer he could grasp from the crowd of voices in his mind. The three small folk that had been watching Millet turned in unison and scurried one after the other through the grass.

"Why not?" Stares-at-moon turned to Heath now, staring him down with its intense beady eyes despite being much closer to the ground than the rabbit was. "Why do your kind tell stories now if you did not tell them then?" Heath sensed that this question was the one that Stares-at-moon had been leading them to, the most important question of the day. He had to admit it was a very good question, one he had never considered before this very moment. Heath couldn't think of a good answer, but some of his un-rabbit-like thoughts worried that there may not be one. He brushed them aside to consider later and turned his attention back to the long tail at his feet.

"I don't know," Heath said calmly. It was a most familiar phrase on his tongue. "What could possibly have changed in the world to make us tell stories where there were none before?" The long tail stared at Heath for what felt like a long time, scrutinising the rabbit with its black eye, then the red one. Heath held his ground. He didn't understand why he was afraid of this little creature and its questions. The proper rabbit thoughts saw no danger, but the un-rabbit-like thoughts had been upset by the interrogation. Some of his thoughts wanted to run and hide, but his other thoughts knew there would be no point. You can't run from a question, it follows you wherever you go.

Stares-at-moon seemed satisfied, if slightly disappointed, with Heath's reply.

"If you don't know then I suppose I will have to show you," it said. "When you've finished stuffing yourselves, shall you take me home? It's not very far for big legs like yours, and there is a task that needs doing." Heath and Millet resumed eating quickly, still watching the sky and listening as they did so. Heath briefly wondered whether it might be impolite for them to eat while the long tail was obviously not doing so, but hunger silenced the un-rabbit-like thoughts. He set about filling his growling stomach.

"What is this task you'd have us do?" Heath asked between mouthfuls.

"Does it truly matter when you've promised to do it anyway?" retorted the long tail, washing its face with its paws in Heath's shadow.

"We don't know what it is we've promised," Heath said. "I'm curious."

"Ah," mused Stares-at-moon. "Curiosity. A wonderful trait. Do you know, fluffy-butt, what they say about curiosity?"

"No," Heath replied, tilting his head to listen better to the peculiar creature.

"It kills cats!" squeaked the long tail with delight, clapping its little hands together, "A most useful thing! Curiosity should be encouraged in everyone!"

"And who says that?" Heath wondered. He'd certainly never heard the phrase, much less had any idea what a cat was.

"Why 'They' do," Stares-at-moon explained without making the point any clearer.

"And who are 'They'?" asked Millet. Stares-at-moon gestured around them, to the angular structures between the trees and the stone banks behind them. Its eyes twinkled with glee.

"They made these things. They shaped the world and put things here."

"Like the Great Stonecutter Rabbit?" Millet asked. Stares-at-moon tilted its head and stared at her.

"I have never heard of a Stonecutter Rabbit," it said, "But They left behind many things for us."

"Left behind?" Heath asked. "Where did they go?"

"One of the big mysteries," Stares-at-moon conceded. "I do not know where they went, only what they left for us. Take me home and I shall show you."

"Okay then," Heath agreed. He decided finding some shelter would be wise. They'd been out in the open far too long. His belly was full, but he wouldn't be happy until he and his sister were safely underground.

"Which way is it?" Stares-at-moon grabbed tufts of Heath's fur, and before the rabbit realised had scampered up onto his back, clinging to his shoulders behind his ears.

"That way!" it said, pointing. Heath froze. He'd never had something sitting on his back before. Part of him wanted to panic while the rest of him, the un-rabbit-like part he assumed, tried to remain reasonable. Of course the long tail would be slowest. It made sense for him to be carried if they were going to move faster. It was just so invasive to have something clutching to his back.

"Are you going to run or sit here all day, fluffy-butt?" it said from his back, disconcertingly close to his ears. Heath shook off his hesitation, careful not to shake off his passenger, and headed off in the desired direction, the long tail clinging happily to his back.

Stares-at-moon guided them back the way they had come, parallel to the stone banks. It urged them to cross the unsettling black streak of stone, burning hot underfoot from baking in the sun, and onto the other side. Despite its assurance neither rabbit was trusting enough to pass under the raised heaps that dotted the black ground, where it would apparently be cooler. The black stone felt rougher than the grey, with occasional white streaks spaced regularly through the black, almost like footprints. If they were footprints Heath didn't recognise the creature they belonged to, but realised it must be very big. It smelled like nothing he knew, but carried overtones of acid and old blood. Only small grasses and weeds grew in the cracks. Crossing the black stone made Heath uneasy, and he was glad when they reached the other side. Here regular patches of respectable grass and short trees grew evenly spaced between the almost ubiquitous grey stone. The rabbits darted from the shelter of one tree to another, aware that dusk would be upon them soon. It was a relief to have real grass under his feet even if it was only for brief periods of time. He wondered how far down the grey stone would go, whether it lurked everywhere under the dirt, like it had been under the mud in the canal.

The weight of the long tail was not as cumbersome as Heath expected it to be at this slow pace. He didn't know how he would cope if he had to run or if it would matter. He wasn't certain he would be able to sprint in any case if it came to it. Heath tried not to show any weakness from the wound in his hip though the long tail couldn't have failed to notice it when it climbed onto him.

"There," said Stares-at-moon, clinging firmly to Heath's shoulders. "Turn through there." Heath turned in the direction he thought the long tail gestured. Two slabs of tall, oddly patterned, red rocks rose from the familiar grey stone. They were distinctly red with predictable streaks of grey woven between them. The pattern was far too regular for Heath's liking, like the scales on a skink, but with no round edges at all. Clumps of greenery peeked out from behind them.

"Past those rocks?" Heath asked.

"Yes," urged the long tail. "It's called a fence. My home is behind them." Hesitantly, Heath stepped around the corner, Millet close behind him.

The plants here were greener than Heath ever remembered seeing. Tall strappy grasses dominated the borders of the area, shading most of the ground. Low grasses filled the centre, but small wildflowers sprung up between them; many varieties Heath couldn't recognise. A single tree stood tall above it all. Its smooth white trunk flecked with black was much narrower than the Great Eucalypt of home. Somehow it still seemed to fill and dominate this space like the Eucalypt had filled the sky. Its leaves were tiny jagged triangles of pale green, fading to yellow, many of which carpeted the ground at its base. The air was cooler on this side of the fence than it had been out in the open. The warm breeze carried the comforting scent of growing plants.

"Your home is beautiful," Millet gasped as she looked around in awe.

"Thank-you," replied Stares-at-moon, climbing down from Heath's shoulders with somewhat less care than Heath would have liked, "but you've not even seen it yet." It scampered between the grasses and up onto a stone ledge in front of a wooden slab.

"Come on," it urged. "Come in before night falls." Millet followed him quickly while Heath took an extra moment to glance around. The plants were so different from home. Had they really travelled this far?

But there, on the edge of the grass, grew the familiar bright yellow of a dandelion. *Well,* he told himself reassuringly, *some things don't change.*

On the stone ledge was a tall, broad, upright slab of decaying wood, oddly straight but clearly weathered. It had a strange scent that Heath wasn't familiar with.

Stares-at-moon squeezed between the wood and adjacent stone, disappearing into the gloomy cavern beyond.

"Come on in!" it urged from inside. Millet and Heath exchanged a worried glance. *Why couldn't it have been a burrow,* Heath lamented to himself.

"We've come this far," Millet reminded him. She jumped onto the ledge and pushed her nose at the hole Stares-at-moon had crawled through. The weathered wooden slab gave way to her pushing, swinging away slightly as she passed through, then creaking back into place. Heath listened after she vanished from sight. Her footsteps became softer in there, but he heard no warning thump as she hopped about. He pulled himself up on the ledge to follow her, slipping slightly on his wounded leg. He righted himself and pushed against the hole. The wooden slab was heavier than his sister had made it seem, but it swung gently for him as he entered.

Listen. Don't listen to me, just listen.

The ground was soft beneath his feet, like a fur-lined burrow, with a strange damp, musty smell and empty moth cocoons scattered all around him. It was dim inside, but compared to the darkness of the stone burrow he could still see quite clearly. All sounds were muffled by the soft ground underfoot.

"Welcome to my home," said Stares-at-moon proudly. "Come this way."

Heath considered his surroundings carefully. The cavern was tall, easily as tall as the stone burrow had been. There was no reasonable way a creature as small as the long tail would have built or hollowed out this place. Tall tunnels branched off the cavern they were in now. A strange substance lined the walls; part wood, part something like white dried mud that had crumbled with damp long ago.

Stares-at-moon happily shuffled its way through the tall tunnels. Part of Heath's mind wondered if the Great Stonecutter Rabbit lived here, but this place didn't feel like a rabbit's home to him. It was so hard and closed and angular. Surely a great rabbit that could dig through stone would find somewhere more suitable? Surely a Stonecutter Rabbit would make short work of these angular tunnels and turn them into something rounder and more comfortable.

They were led to a chamber with three large objects that appeared to be more angular boulders, but were actually quite soft when Heath leant against one. Judging by the holes chewed into them, either the small folk or the long tail itself probably burrowed into them to nest.

Scattered on the soft, dry ground were yet more angular objects. They looked like flaps from a paperbark tree stacked on top of each other though the patterns were different and far too regular. It was almost like the flight feathers of a bird folded into a wing. Stares-at-moon scampered over one of them and stroked it fondly.

"Do you know what this is?" it asked them. Heath gazed around the chamber, with its strange shapes and materials.

"No, I don't know," he replied with complete honesty.

"They called them books," Stares-at-moon said, clear awe in its tone. "They tell stories. Wonderful stories. Stories about the world, about Them, about us. Stories from long ago in a different time."

"Who are They?" Millet asked. The long tail gestured around the two rabbits, staring with wonder and concern at the chamber they stood in.

"They. Them. The tall folk. The makers. Whatever name you call them by, or don't, as the case may be. These were their homes. These were their books." Heath sat on his haunches and considered the long tail's reverent words. He'd never heard of tall folk, of makers or whatever their names might be. It had always just been rabbits and their ways since the first stories had been told.

Yet here, according to the long tail, were more stories. Stories from creatures long ago and long gone. Perhaps they could answer the questions that no rabbit had dared to ask yet. Perhaps they would hold the truth.

"What do they say?" he asked, peering over Stares-at-moon's shoulders at the markings on the page. Rabbits had always told stories, it was part of warren life. They passed from one rabbit to another, sharing tales deep in their burrows. A rabbit may die, but the stories carried on so long as there was someone to listen. To find stories pinned down on an object was an unsettling thought. These were stories of the dead.

They must have been important to be preserved like this.

"So many things," the long tail crooned, stroking the pages before it with care, "and pictures too, that we might see as they saw." Small black marks adorned most of the page, but in one corner was a blending of colours and shapes that made no sense to Heath's eyes. It was not unlike the coloured marks on the grey banks near the stone burrow. Stares-at-moon, however, apparently understood them very well. *Maybe it's his red eye*, Heath thought to himself, *maybe They had red eyes and that's how it understands those marks. After all, you need proper ears to hear proper sounds. Perhaps you need the right eye to see the right things.*

"This here is the terrible dragon," said Stares-at-moon, caressing the marks in front of them, "with his long tail and burning belly. He has hard scales to protect himself and fire in his mouth. A most terrible, fearsome beast, and yet the stories say he holds wisdom for the brave heroes that outwit him." The long tail struggled to flip over the page. Millet stepped forward to nudge her nose under the corner and help.

"Here, the dryad," Stares-at-moon continued, gesturing to the indecipherable markings before it. "They turn into trees and back again. Many is the hero who has been fooled by them, the book says." Millet helped him turn the next cluster of pages, stuck together with old damp.

"And here, look at the phoenix!" Stares-at-moon squealed with growing excitement at the red and orange page. "A great bird with feathers of fire!" Heath suddenly began to pay more attention. *Maybe the hawk knew of the phoenix?* There were more books scattered on the surrounding ground, some opened and flipped through long ago. Little footprints tracked across their open pages. *Do all of them tell such stories? How can one mind remember them all?* Stares-at-moon lifted a few more pages at a time, and Millet would obligingly nudge them across with her nose. She seemed just as intrigued as Heath was.

"Ah hah! A personal favorite of mine. Vicious claws, a thirst for blood and love of riddles. It will tear apart the foolish hero that cannot beat it in a game of wits." Stares-at-moon mimed clawing at the air in enthusiasm.

"What's that?" Heath asked, cocking his head.

"The riddling sphinx!" Stares-at-moon gleefully exclaimed.

"No, I mean what's a riddle?" Heath clarified. "Is it another creature?"

The long tail scampered up to him, rose on its hind legs and stared at him intently over its long nose and whiskers.

"The more of it there is, the less you see," it said. Heath blinked, suddenly unsure of himself.

"What?"

"The more of it there is, the less you see," Stares-at-moon repeated. "It's a riddle. Think about it. Find the answer in your head."

Heath's mind startled into action, scrambled to think of something that was hard to see. He spluttered a little as multiple options presented themselves, but he knew somehow they were all wrong. In the end he fell back to those words he relied on so often, yet hated saying.

"I don't know."

Stares-at-moon patted him on the nose consolingly.

"That's okay fluffy-butt, you've got time to think."

Heath backed up, fleeing the invasion of his personal space. There was certainly a lot to think about, more than he could handle at one time. Part of him wanted to run. The other part of him knew you couldn't outrun thoughts. He chased the one thought that stood out from the others.

"But are these things real?"

"Of course they're real!" Stares-at-moon insisted, throwing its paws up in the air. "Why would They have written something that was not truth?"

"But how do you know?" Heath insisted, accustomed to believing his own eyes and the words of other rabbits rather than the marks of the mysterious They. "I mean you, Stares-at-moon, yourself." The long tail stepped back and puffed out its little grey chest with pride.

"For I have seen one," it declared proudly, "With my own wise eyes." It tapped the white crescent of fur on its forehead. It scurried back to the book, lifted a few pages over its head and scurried beneath them.

"Here! This one!" It declared excitedly. Millet nosed under the pages and delicately levered them over.

"The unicorn," Stares-at-moon whispered with awe. The rabbits crowded around the book, watching the long tail stroke the marks on the page. Heath wasn't quite sure what he was looking at, but there seemed to be a lot of white.

"The blessed unicorn," Stares-at-moon continued, breathlessly excited. "Light of foot and white as the streak on my face. Two toes on each foot, and a tail like the lion, but the most distinctive feature is the single great horn that rises from its head. The magical horn, to heal the sick and cure disease. Oh such a wonderful thing." Stares-at-moon turned to stare Heath in the eye, "The book says that the unicorn will only appear to those heroes who are brave and pure of heart. They must be true and fair and never falter. Yes indeed, one must be a pretty darn good hero to find the unicorn. And I have seen it." The little long tail was clearly very proud of itself. Millet's eyes grew wide.

"Really? Where?" she asked. Stares-at-moon tapped its long nose with an air of conspiracy.

"The unicorn walks through the gardens in her own time," it said. "Mostly she ignores the small folk, but takes care to never step upon them. Isn't that right?" Stares-at-moon looked up. In the shelves above them, the holes in the walls, on every surface overlooking them sat small folk, watching silently. They nodded their heads in synchrony, answering the long tail's question.

Heath's fur bristled. He hadn't heard any of them come in. Millet crouched, looking up at all the small folk staring down on them.

"And, um," she whispered, curiosity getting the better of her. "What's a lion?" Stares-at-moon shrugged.

"There is another creature in the book with the head of a lion," he offered. "But no lion itself."

"And no tail?" Millet asked.

"No," it admitted, "but there's no mistaking the unicorn when you see her." Heath felt uneasy under the gaze of the small folk. There were more of them than he could count, all the same soft brown colour. He didn't know how many others there might be and didn't like their profound silence. Admittedly they had not so far wished them any harm, in fact they owed the small folk their lives. However a creature that he couldn't hear was not a creature he wanted to be around, whatever their motive may be.

"And what's a hero?" Heath asked, trying to ignore the fact that he and his sister were surrounded "You've mentioned them a few times. What are they?"

"No idea," the long tail shrugged. "They're mentioned often, but the book doesn't have an entry for them. Hopefully one of the other books will enlighten us, which brings us to your task." A chorus of chattering squeaks erupted from the audience of small folk seated around the room.

"What is the task you wish us to do?" Heath asked, trying to focus on the present and not the rising urge to flee.

"Oh yes," said Stares-at-moon, as though it had completely slipped its mind. "They want more books." Heath tilted his head.

"And where do we get them from?" he wondered. Stares-at-moon scurried across the chamber to a depression in the wall. It climbed up and gestured to the bark-like columns within it.

"These are more books," it said, "Sitting here, stored away. They look like nothing like this. But once they're open, oh the stories they will tell." It grabbed hold with its nimble fingers and climbed up the spine of the books, dragging its tail behind it. It perched on top of them.

"They're right here for us," Stares-at-moon continued, "but

they're packed in too tightly for us to push out. They need to be pulled." The small folk watched silently.

"If you big creatures, such as you are, can pull them out for us, all that effort in chewing up the ivy might be considered worthwhile."

"You want us to pull out the books?" checked Millet.

"You said you can dig," the long tail reminded them. "Dig out our books." Millet stepped up to the vertically stacked books and scratched between them. Stares-at-moon watched from above the books, and the small folk stared from their vantage points around the room.

"I can only get a little hold," she said. "Can you grab it higher?"

Heath reached above her to grab the dusty book spine with his teeth. Millet grabbed it from below. It felt like soft bark under fur in his mouth, dry, crumbly and tasteless. They heaved together, Heath reaching up to place his paws either side of the book.

"Almost there fluffy-butts!" Stares-at-moon urged. "Almost there!" Slowly the book slid towards them, their sharp teeth sinking into the spine. Heath backed up, his hind feet slipping off the ledge. Suddenly he was falling backward quicker than he had anticipated. He and the book tumbled backwards, over Millet's head. They landed with a thud, the book on top of them both. He caught his breath and wiggled out from under the book. Millet backed out from underneath it, looking startled, but she didn't run. The books either side of the one they had dislodged leaned into the gap they had made.

Above them, the small folk squeaked in delight. Stares-at-moon clapped merrily.

"Well done fluffy-butts!"

"What does it say?" Millet asked, staring keenly at the open pages.

"No idea," replied the long tail. "They take time to read. I'll do that later." It tapped the books it was sitting on with a paw. "Now pull these out and leave them open for me. I shall decipher their knowledge in the coming days."

The two rabbits worked as darkness fell to heave the books one by one onto the floor. They spread them out so Stares-at-moon could browse through them at the long tail's leisure. The ground was covered in books when they had finished, and the scent of moths filled the air. The small folk slowly crept away as silently as they had arrived. Heath had barely noticed until now that most of them had already gone.

"Well now," said Stares-at-moon, "Today has been a productive day. And what will you two fluffy-butts do now?"

"We need to go home," said Heath. He had to admit he was quite tired. "We don't know the way though."

"Do you know how we can get home?" asked Millet, "We live in a warren under the Great Eucalypt on a hill. It's grass all around, as far as you can see."

"Or it was, until the fire," Heath reminded her.

"I travel nowhere near far enough to know where that is," said Stares-at-moon. "Grass as far as you can see. Imagine that." It tapped its little fingers against its chin, "There's never anything as far as you can see here. The grass is always fenced in by walls or stone."

"I suppose we'll have to follow the banks back to the Stonecutter Rabbit's burrow," Heath decided, "Home must be in that direction, somewhere."

"The unicorn would know," Stares-at-moon suggested. "I'm sure we can find her tomorrow."

"Oh, oh yes let's!" chirped Millet, apparently thrilled by the prospect. She seemed far too happy in Heath's opinion, who only felt weary now.

"Well, if she'll know our way home, I don't see why not," he agreed.

"Or," said Stares-at-moon, yawning, "you could stay around here. There are other books in other caverns. We could use some strong fluffy-butts to pull them out."

"But we need our warren," Heath explained. "We're not...we're not really rabbits without our warren."

"Well there's two of you," the long tail noted, "and two can quickly become six and six become many more if you set your mind to it, if you know what I mean." The two rabbits stared at each other. They did know exactly what it meant, but neither had ever considered the possibility.

"I'm not..." Millet stammered.

"We're not," Heath finished for her.

"Well it was an idea," sighed Stares-at-moon. "I'll help you find the unicorn tomorrow, if that's what you wish."

"Can't we start tonight?" asked Millet.

"The unicorn prefers daylight," Stares-at-moon replied, "and so do I. Less death on wings. Sleep well, fluffy-butts." With that the long tail turned and disappeared into a hole in the soft mounds that dominated the room.

The rabbits curled up in a soft corner of the cavern after pulling the more comfortable pieces of debris around them to make a temporary nest. It was more comfortable than the muddy hollow they had last slept in, but not the warm, fur lined burrow Heath was longing for. At least there were no mosquitoes here to pester him, and he was fairly sure there were small folk watching out for them. They were impossible to hear, but he occasionally caught a flicker of movement or a twinkle of an eye to suggest that they waited in the periphery of the room. Watching.

He did not sleep well. Even though they were likely safer among the books than they had been at the bottom of the stoney banks, his heart and mind would not settle. Both still raced.

He dreamed of the warren, the storm and the flames. In his dream the hawk was wreathed in fire, not just carrying it. It always seemed to be in front of him, rising from the surrounding flames no matter which way he turned.

"You're mine," it hissed through smoke and ash. "You're mine."

He woke suddenly as light crept into the cavern. A brief moment of panic rose in his heart. He wasn't underground. He wasn't safe.

Then yesterday's memories returned to him, complex though they were.

Millet sat nearby, cleaning herself. She had removed all but the faintest touch of dust from her coat after the gruelling last few days.

"You slept a long time," she noted. "Are you alright?" Heath licked his paws and rubbed his face to wake quicker.

"I suppose I'm more tired than I thought," he confessed. He had no intention of telling his sister about the dream. Rabbits, as a whole didn't know what to make of dreams. Some thought they were lost stories from the past. Some believed they were stories yet to be told, waiting to come true. A few believed they were complete nonsense. Heath hoped for nonsense. Millet hopped back towards him.

"We can feed outside," she suggested. "Stares-at-moon hasn't come out of the hole yet." She paused, regarding her brother critically for a moment.

"Your eyes look swollen," she told him. "Are you sure you're alright?"

"Just tired I think," Heath replied, "or perhaps the mud in my eyes from yesterday. Some grass would do us both good." The two rabbits made their way back out to the shaded grassy entrance. They wandered outside with little difficulty and set about eating their fill amongst the shelter of the plants.

Light dew had settled on the leaves overnight, welcome moisture before the inevitable heat of the coming day. Heath ate slowly, picking the tenderest blades of grass, always keeping an eye on his surroundings. His lips felt different, a little puffy, which made it difficult to pick the grass as he usually would have. There were dandelions here, fresh and yellow and comforting in the way they reminded him of home. The grass here did not taste like the grass at the warren, it was oddly sweeter. Still, it felt good simply to be able to graze in relative safety.

"You're up early, fluffy-butts." Stares-at-moon sat on the

ledge by the entrance, stifling a yawn. "Ready for your adventures? Won't you have stories to tell, back at your warren."

"Yes," Millet chirped enthusiastically, "if our warren believes us. It sounds wonderful to meet a unicorn." Stares-at-moon chuckled.

"It's not just wonder that awaits on a journey," it reminded her, "but if you're both ready, we shall find whatever awaits us."

I will keep the colour of your eyes.

Stares-at-moon rode contentedly on Heath's shoulders once more, having made itself quite comfortable on that vantage point. For some reason the long tail's weight seemed so much harder to bear today, but Heath said nothing. They needed directions else they'd likely end up wandering through this hard grey maze for the rest of their lives.

Millet would scout ahead through one patch or clearing at a time, and then keep watch while they caught up to her. The scenery varied very little, always hard angular structures walling in diverse clearings of plants, squares of greenery breaking through the hard grey stone wherever they could. Sometimes they would come across a plant he recognised, but they rarely stopped long enough for him to savour it. Millet would eat mouthfuls of grass while waiting for Heath and his passenger to catch up. Heath himself found it hard to grab a bite between sprints, but also found he was more preoccupied with his thoughts than his stomach. Perhaps it was excitement, or perhaps it was an undercurrent of fear.

"I have been meaning to ask you something," he ventured at last, quizzing his passenger.

"I imagine you have a great many questions," Stares-at-moon replied, "even if you do not yet know them all." The long tail began to list points, tapping its fingers one by one as it counted.

"Why is the sky blue? Where did these structures come from? What were They like? Where are They now? Why do some creatures eat plants and yet others must eat meat? Shall I go on?" Heath paused for a moment, waiting for a signal from his sister.

"They are certainly good questions," he conceded, "but they are not the one I had in mind. Perhaps you can answer the other questions later?" The long tail chuckled, as it often did.

"No fluffy-butt, I cannot answer those questions later. That is rather their point. So out with it, what is the question you would ask of me?" Heath hesitated. Compared to the questions of Stares-at-moon, his question seemed so small and mundane. He was almost embarrassed.

"Why do you have white fur streaking down your face?" he finally asked. "And your red eye? If you don't mind me asking, that is. None of the small folk had any white, and I've never seen it on a rabbit." He had half expected the long tail to laugh again. Instead, Stares-at-moon seemed to take him seriously. Heath wondered if the seriousness was worse.

"It's their mark," it whispered so only Heath could hear, which was not difficult to do considering how close it was to his head. "They are unknowable. They may give and they may take, but they always leave a mark. This, the moon in my fur, is mine. This eye they gave me grants me the knowing of the words in the books. Those small folk are glad of the reading though they can't yet grasp the words themselves. They cannot wield the words. They can only listen. Listen and sing."

"Are the small folk your children?" Heath wondered. *After all,* he thought, *they do look very similar.*

"Oh no," Stares-at-moon corrected him. "They're all well grown. They're not long tails. They are their own kind of folk, fluffy-butt." Heath considered this for a moment before spotting Millet's signal and dashing across the open ground to her next hiding place.

"Then where are your folk?" It seemed like the next logical question.

"Oh my," Stares-at-moon chuckled again at last. "They are everywhere. In every corner of the land we are, though you may not see us. The better question to ask would be where aren't my folk?"

"Okay. Where are they not?" Heath asked obligingly.

"Wherever I am," Stares-at-moon sighed and fell silent. Heath sensed that was the end of that line of questioning. Still he did not understand what Stares-at-moon meant by calling his white fur 'Their mark'. He supposed he understood very little in this place. At least at home, in the warren, he had understood his place, his duties and the expectations upon him. He understood the changing day there, the plants and the soil.

There were still uncertainties about his life at the warren. His fate would be uncertain when he left for a warren of his own. An ambiguous future was at least one thing that never changed.

Millet hopped cautiously along an exposed grey clearing, ears alert and eyes on the sky.

"You said the small folk don't grasp words, yet," Heath thought out loud. "Does that mean you expect they will, one day?" Stares-at-moon ruffled the fur between Heath's ears playfully.

"Well spotted fluffy-butt, well spotted," it said. "I tell you this in truth, make what you will of it. There was a morning when small folk and long tails alike walked these lands with no care for questions, no interest in words, no understanding of Them. We lived simply, survived cleverly, and every morning was a new day. Then, one night, the dust fell from the sky. They vanished. When we awoke, we truly awoke, and began to ask questions. We had words. We had ideas. We asked bigger questions every day. Now the small folk, they have been slower to come to questions. They do not ask them so loudly, but they do wonder. They take those questions in like a thirsty soul takes in water. And you know what I think, fluffy-butt?" The long tail waited a moment for Heath to answer. It was a ludicrous thing. How could Heath possibly know what another was thinking, least of all Stares-at-moon. "I believe one day, when they grasp the words in their little mouths, they won't just be asking questions. They'll be spluttering answers." Ahead of them, Millet hid herself in long grass around a gnarly old bottlebrush shrub. Heath scanned the area, caution always prudent, before making his way through the open. *What an odd sight I must be*, he mused, *with this long tail on my back*. The weight of Stares-at-moon was starting to seriously slow him down now, and his aching hip was definitely not getting the rest it needed to heal. It felt like forever, being out in the open, but Heath and his passenger eventually reached the next spot of cover.

"Sister," he whispered in the tall grass, "I need to rest. Soon." Millet sniffed him worriedly. He was sweating badly with exertion, moisture they certainly didn't want to lose in the heat of Summer. It was bound to attract the blowflies.

"Would it help if I carried Stares-at-moon?" she offered. Heath shook his head. She was already smaller than he was, carrying the long tail would slow her more than it slowed him. In any case he felt that lightening his burden would not be enough. He needed to rest.

"There's bound to be a garden to rest in," said Stares-at-moon. "You've carried me this far, my little legs could use a stretch. Let me down while you stay here. I'll see what's beyond those walls."

The long tail slipped down from Heath's shoulders and scurried across the stony surfaces to disappear around a corner of crumbled yellow stone. Heath lay down for a moment. The weight off his shoulders was a relief, but he badly needed a long rest and lie down. He wasn't used to carrying something, or someone, on his back. Now he thought about it, he couldn't recall another rabbit having carried a passenger on its shoulders. What a story they would have to tell when they reached home. He wondered what the other rabbits would think.

"They must have been very big creatures," Millet mused, "and very strong to have emptied all those dens." She shook her head to dislodge the blowfly that had already discovered them.

"Where do you think they went?" she wondered.

"I don't–" Heath began, and Millet joined him on the last word, "–know." He stared at her, taken aback.

"I didn't expect you to know," she told him playfully. "I thought you might just have an idea. How could you possibly know for certain where they went?" Heath repressed the urge to say 'I don't know' again.

"Does it matter? They're not here now," he replied.

"When you know a fox has been, but isn't here now, does that matter?" she asked, but continued before giving him a chance to answer her. "What if They come back one day?"

Heath remained silent, unwilling to confess his lack of knowledge and be mocked once more. He didn't have the energy for these games.

"We'll deal with it when it happens," he told her.

"What if they're not gone?" she pressed, happily following her own line of thought, "What if they've migrated? They might be back any day."

"I don't think They flew," Heath told her.

"Why not?" Millet wondered, "How can we possibly know?" Heath looked around, trying to gather his thoughts coherently.

"Everything here is placed for creatures to walk. The pathways are easy to navigate. I doubt a flying creature would care for such things." He stretched, trying to follow his ideas while they came together.

"And I think They've been gone for some time. There's no scent, no scats, no prints. Otherwise I'm sure Stares-at-moon would have pointed them out already. I doubt they're coming back."

"Must be very nice or very dull to be so sure," Millet muttered. Heath thumped his foot angrily.

"A moment ago you mocked me for not knowing, and now you mock me for thinking I do?" he demanded. "Whatever game you're playing, at least tell me the rules." His sister looked him up and down.

"You're not normally this mean," she noted. "Are you sure you're well?"

"Hoi, fluffy-butts!" Stares-at-moon called as it came scampering back. "Found you some grass and shade. Walls all around, no sharp-toothed beasties sneaking about. Nice place for a nap. Follow me, quick now."

Stares-at-moon guided the rabbits over a crumbled pile of debris between the foreboding walls. Long seedy grasses scrambled for space in the rubble and the scent of wildflowers wafted around them. The sun was harsh, and only the faintest wisps of clouds drifted in from the horizon. It was foolish for them to be out in the open in such heat, but it would be foolish for a predator as well.

More blowflies arrived, attracted by the movement. They never seemed far away. The rabbits rounded the corner of the cavernous structure to discover a meadow, still lush despite the dry summer. Their noses flooded with heady scents of flowering plants and fragrant leaves. Heath breathed deeply. He'd never smelt anything quite like it.

"A nice little spot, eh?" said Stares-at-moon, looking pleased with itself.

"It looks beautiful," agreed Millet. "It smells delicious." Clambering for space, overflowing from soil contained behind ancient wooden logs, grew countless species of plants with foliage in all kinds of shapes. White and orange butterflies drifted from one bloom to another, completely oblivious to the visitors in their midst.

The rabbits crept cautiously into the meadow, sniffing and tasting individual leaves as they went. They were all so deliciously tempting, each plant different from the next. Stares-at-moon clambered up one of the wooden logs, grabbed a strand of grass covered in golden seeds and dragged it into the shade.

Most of the grass underfoot was the same faintly sweet species that grew near Stares-at-moon's books, but the plants overflowing their wooden barriers were new to Heath. They seemed too inviting, too tempting, to the naturally cautious rabbits, but wonderful at the same time. *Surely others would have told stories of these plants if they had encountered them,* Heath thought to himself. He certainly would be telling others about their delightful tastes if he ever had the chance. There were many flavoured plants and dozens of different coloured flowers to sample, scattered randomly wherever they found space to grow. One vigorous curly leafed plant with a fresh, crisp flavour particularly took Heath's fancy.

"Oh, I wish these grew at home," Millet exclaimed between hurried mouthfuls. Heath ate slowly, his mind wandering. The overgrown grass hid them well in the shade, but obscured their view of any approaching danger.

"All the best plants grow in places like this," Stares-at-moon told her, "I think They placed them here."

"Just for us?" Millet wondered. "How kind of them." The long tail chuckled. Heath felt uneasy. Why would she just assume that the bounty of plants were here for their benefit? The idea sounded far too much like the beliefs of Lantana. He didn't believe for a moment that the world was somehow deliberately designed for their wellbeing. Above their heads a golden spider spun an intricate web between the branches of a short flowering tree. Its yellow legs expertly carried the silken threads behind it as it wove its trap between the white blossoms. Heath regarded it for a moment, but it would be no danger to them.

"I doubt it's just for us, fluffy-butt," Stares-at-moon replied. It helped itself to more seeds from the plants behind it, delicately picking their husks off with his long front teeth. "I wonder if They didn't also enjoy them." The idea that They had placed things in the world for their own reasons, not for the benefit of rabbits, made more sense. The more he thought about it, the less comfort the concept gave him.

"I think I'm starting to like Them," Millet said, continuing to feast. If They had placed plants like these for their own reasons, what else had they placed? Was the stone burrow their creation? If so, why? How could he hope to understand their reasons in shaping the landscape as it was?

"You don't know anything about Them," Heath reminded her.

"I know they told stories and had good plants to eat," Millet disagreed. Another shred of plant rapidly disappeared behind her delicate lips, "That sounds pretty good to me."

"Fine, so you know two things about them," Heath conceded. "Of all the great mysteries and unknowable things in the world, you have understood two of them and somehow you think you have an answer." Above them a white butterfly fluttered into the golden spider's web. It pulled erratically trying to free itself, but only attracted the spider's attention.

"Would you say two things are all you need to know about me?" Heath continued. The plants were good, but something about them left a strange taste on his lips. He didn't know why, but his un-rabbit-like thoughts suspected it was the not knowing that made it worse.

"Yes," Millet retorted, "You're grumpy when you're hungry and you're always a sceptic." She shook a persistent blowfly from her ears and selected a new plant to sample.

"And that's all you need to know about me, is it?" Heath replied, reaching around to lick his wound and chase the flies away. "Not one thing more?"

"Well," she sighed, guilt creeping into her voice, "I suppose some things more."

"Your two points make him sound so mean," Stares-at-moon laughed from its perch above them, a pile of orderly seed husks steadily growing beside it.

"And your two points makes Them sound quite nice," Heath noted. His natural rabbit caution suspected there must be more to Them than it seemed.

"Stares-at-moon, were They nice?" Millet asked, ears pricked forward awaiting the long tail's answer.

"They are unknowable," Stares-at-moon replied casually. "I have spent my life trying to understand them, and haven't yet. Fortunately I shall have many more days to do so."

"Whatever They are, I do know these plants are good." Millet returned to the task at hand and resumed feeding. Above them the struggling butterfly was cocooned by the industrious spider. Heath watched it uneasily, unable to calm the troubled thoughts in the back of his mind.

There was a peculiar pattern this meadow and the plants outside Stares-at-moon's home seemed to follow. The plants were tallest at the edges, in all manner of varieties, but only grasses seemed to thrive in the centre. Within the zones themselves the plants were scattered randomly, but the centre in both places had been mostly open grass. At Stares-at-moon's home there had been a tree in the centre.

Here the centre had grass growing unusually high, mounded up on something. Even though he continued to watch their surroundings for danger, his gaze always returned to the mounded grass in the centre of the meadow.

"Why don't you eat more?" Millet urged him, but Heath paid her little attention. He was certain now that it was the mound of grass causing his unease. He needed to understand why. Cautious rabbits were long lived rabbits.

Heath crept into the centre of the meadow where the long grass piled up particularly thickly.

"Do you see something, fluffy-butt?" Stares-at-moon called. Heath didn't answer. Caution was urging him forward now, the same feeling that made him search the sky when emerging from a burrow, or to sniff the wind every time it changed. Something odd lurked in this grass.

The others watched him as he snuck towards the tussocks, keeping his body tense and low to the ground. The grass here was older, drier, and clinging to something as it scrambled for height. There was no concerning smell, no worrying sound, but still it made him feel uneasy. He didn't like not knowing why his instincts told him to run. You couldn't run from shadows. You needed a direction to flee. He needed to know why, and the need was making him brave.

He clawed his way through the old dry grass as high as possible, pulling away clumps at a time. Nothing leapt out at him. The only noise, other than his efforts, was the soft, dry breeze through the plants and the ever present blowflies.

His claws caught on something fine, but strong. It gave a little under his weight, but did not tear. Quickly he pulled away more grass to closer examine it.

A narrow, strong material of a reddish brown colour, slightly powdery to touch, bent under his weight, but wouldn't tear no matter how he tried. It was woven around more pieces of itself into hexagons like a thick spider web encasing the area under the grass. The closer he looked the more of it there seemed to be. It stretched over the entirety of the mound, bordered by crumbling, brittle wooden frames at either end. It even stretched along the ground inside, he saw more weaving in the same regular pattern between the old grass that had pushed its way up between it.

Some sort of web, he thought to himself, *but what sort of fly must it be here to catch?*

He couldn't reach the overgrown matted grass inside to move it, nor could he break through the web. He satisfied his curiosity and growing dread by finding a new angle to remove the grass and peek in.

By one edge he saw a raised circular object. It was shiny like the full moon and curved so that water or dew had gathered in it once, though only a stain remained after the summer heat. There was something else there too that Heath didn't quite recognise. It was white, as white as the fur on Stares-at-moon's face, but looked hard, like a rock. *No, not a rock,* he realised, *more like an egg. It's fragile. Delicate. Detailed.* The object had complex depressions and protrusions that Heath couldn't quite make sense of. There were similar smaller objects nearby, running deeper into the grass thicket in a

straight line.
He didn't understand until he saw the teeth.

We are not always what we seem ...

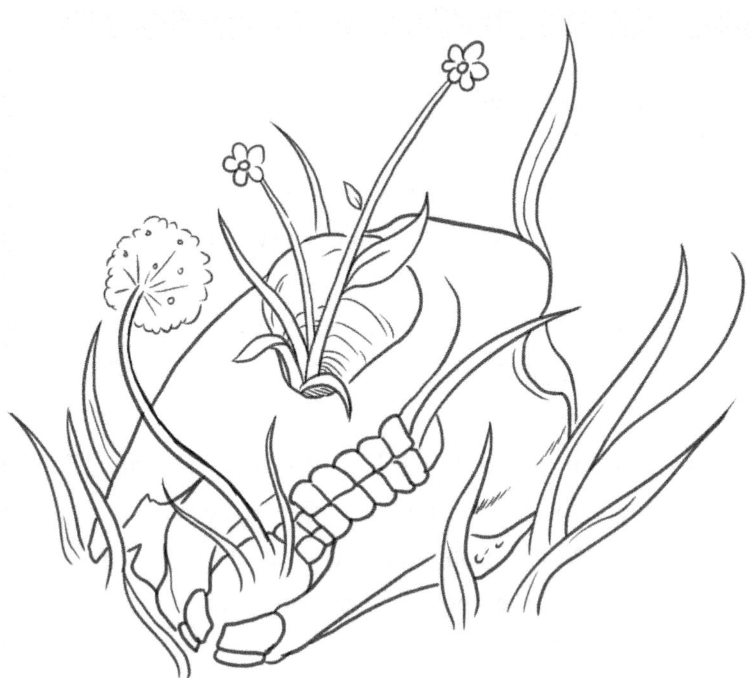

One end of the object had a pair of sharp cutting teeth, so like the teeth he often saw when disciplined by older rabbits in the warren. Teeth like those in his own head.

The object was the right size to be a rabbit head, stripped of its fur and flesh. It was completely clean, and devoid of scent. However it had become trapped, it happened long ago. He had seen no other signs of rabbits on their journey, and this was not an encouraging one. Whatever had ensnared this poor soul, perhaps it waited to snare another.

Perhaps that was the purpose of all the delicious plants here, to attract other rabbits. To trick them. To trap them. To lull their natural caution away and make them easy prey for whatever it was that had lurked here. Whether it remained or not, this was not a safe place for them to be, tempting though it was.

He backed away slowly, looking carefully at where he placed his feet. A rabbit could easily grow fat on the abundant plants here, but that was not a prudent thing to do. When clear of the trap, he sprinted back to Millet as fast as his injury would allow him.

"What did you see?" she asked, mildly suspicious on reading his body language, but still enjoying the diverse and plentiful food around her.

"Enough to know we should leave," he stated firmly. "This is no safe place for rabbits. It's never been. There is a trap, and a dead soul." Millet dropped her mouthful of food. Stares-at-moon sounded rather less concerned and continued to eat the seeds in front of it.

"There are long dead souls to be found all over the place," it stated, cheeks bulging with food. "The dead won't try to eat you fluffy-butt."

"The dead shouldn't be ignored," Heath insisted. "We don't

even know how they died. But if whatever wishes death upon our kind might return here, I want to be far away." Millet was alert now, he could almost imagine her frantic heart pumping in her little chest.

"Let's leave," she agreed. With a sigh Stares-at-moon climbed down from its seat and clambered back onto Heath's shoulders.

"Very well," it said, "but you fluffy-butts don't recognise a good thing when you see it."

They travelled back towards their path, neither rabbit liking the idea of staying where another had so mysteriously died. Heath's thoughts scrambled for something solid to hold onto. There had been no smell of death, blood or disease. Everything had seemed so clean, so peaceful.

So deceptive.

It must have been some kind of trap. That was the only conclusion his mind would reach. He understood spiders wove their webs in areas the flies would often visit, waiting for them to stumble into their sticky strands. The webs never seemed tough to a rabbit, but they were many times bigger than a fly.

Perhaps it was a much bigger spider that had lurked in that meadow. Perhaps They were like spiders, placing their plants carefully to lure careless rabbits into their clutches. Otherwise perhaps the web-maker wandered in after They left, taking advantage of the tempting plants. Heath shuddered. It was definitely best to be far from than place.

Stares-at-moon felt the shudder beneath him.

"Upset, fluffy-butt?" the long tail asked him, its tone

distinctly more relaxed than Heath was. "You can't go getting upset every time you find a pile of bones. The dead are all over the place." Both rabbits paused in their tracks.

"What do you mean?" Heath asked softly, fear creeping in to his voice. His mind assessed every possible path as an escape route, but if nowhere was safe then where should they run?

"Oh," Stares-at-moon explained, far too casually, "You can find the bones all over the place. Mostly inside the homes, sometimes stuck on or in things outside. They don't hurt you, been there a long time, have the dead." The long tail's words did nothing to calm Heath's mind.

"How long?" he asked flatly.

"As long as I remember, and my mamma before me, and her mamma before her." Stares-at-moon scratched an ear, oblivious to the rabbit's stress levels. "Can't tell you much before that though. I dare say the dead outnumber the living many times over."

"What sort of bones?" Millet asked, fear slowly giving way to curiosity.

"Lots of little ones, many with killer teeth inside the buildings. Sometimes feathery ones. All from ages past."

"Did They leave bones behind?" Millet asked. "The makers, or whatever They were?" Heath considered the question. Of course it was a good one, he couldn't have thought of a better one himself. Why hadn't he thought of it before?

"Nope," Stares-at-moon replied, "Not a single one. They did not die as others did. They simply left."

"Left to go where?" Millet asked.

"Just not here," the long tail replied. "Now come along, we're not going to find you a unicorn sitting here in a panic all day, now are we?"

They continued scampering from cover to cover. Heath did not feel as rested as he should have, but he knew he had not felt truly peaceful since they had left the warren. How many days had it been? Two? It felt longer than a lifetime, but he supposed it would. The only other creatures they saw were a few songbirds flying past, a handful of clumsy white butterflies and the ever present blowflies.

He was so sick of blowflies. He longed to be underground again where they wouldn't follow, safe from the heat.

The evening brought a cool change. Radiating heat lifted from the ubiquitous grey stone on the breeze. Parched leaves rustled as the breeze passed. The blowflies began to relent in the cool, but before long mosquitoes would venture forth to satisfy their thirst.

"We'd best find a little nook for the evening," Stares-at-moon suggested. "Wait here while I find a hole we can all scurry into."

"No," said Heath, to the surprise of both the long tail and his sister, "I don't want your holes. I don't want your caverns where things have died. I want the soft earth around me, just trees and grass and fur. I want nothing of your precious 'They'. This is no place for rabbits. It's not right for us." He thumped his foot once for emphasis. He wasn't sure how the words bubbled up so quickly, but he knew their truth as soon as he spoke them.

"Are you okay?" Millet asked, her soft voice full of concern.

"No, no I really don't think I am," Heath replied, "and this place, these unknowable things don't help."

"Well what do you want then?" huffed Stares-at-moon from his shoulders.

"Somewhere quiet, open," Heath said, "with soft soil and shade. Real soil, not that furry strange stuff around the books. And not mud either."

"If you know so much then, you go find it," Stares-at-moon snapped. Heath shook himself, forcing the long tail to cling tightly to his fur. Without another word Heath set off towards the freshest smelling air he could sense. Millet followed not far behind him. He moved away from the stony structures and their strange mix of plants, seeking open familiar grass and trees. He knew Millet worried about him. It was silly for her to waste thoughts and energy on him though, given that they had so many other things to worry about in their circumstances.

He followed his nose, crossed the hot black ground and headed for open air. Millet would stop and scan the sky, but Heath trudged on, determined. Stares-at-moon muttered to itself on his back.

The ground sloped down in front of him, not the slippery smooth grey slopes of the stone burrow, but the accommodating grass covered slopes of trustworthy earth. Ahead he spied clusters of small trees and bushes with faintly familiar smells. Nothing like the Great Eucalypt of home, but closer than anything else had been here.

He wandered among the small trees. Any one of them could have fit inside the chamber with Stares-at-moon's books. None towered over him. None felt truly right, but they did feel better. They each clustered in groups of about half a dozen grown trees, with little saplings popping up in between. No grass grew around the trees, but it did grow in wide paths between the clusters. He still didn't feel comfortable, but it was an improvement.

"Yes," muttered Stares-at-moon, dragging out the syllables in a tone Heath was not certain was sincere. "No shelter, no comforts, but lots of sticks and bark. Isn't this just lovely." Rabbits did not have a word for pouting. If they were to continue associating with Stares-at-moon however, they were going to need one. Heath looked around for a place to make their burrow.

And there, when he needed it most, was a golden dandelion flower.

"This way," he announced. He chose a nearby thicket of the scraggly trees and set about exploring their roots. Old branches had fallen from them and made a loose barrier underneath that they squeezed through. Stares-at-moon clung tightly to Heath.

The largest tree of the thicket had exposed roots, thick and gnarly. Its twisted grey bark split and cracked along its length creating tiny crevices for beetles and spiders to hide in. Its leaves were narrow and faintly furry, still green despite the heat. Reddish flower buds grew along its stalks but had not yet bloomed to brave the harsh summer. Leaf litter and bark covered the ground but the soil was cool and loamy below.

"This will do," Heath decided. "This will do nicely." He began scratching twigs, bark and leaf litter away from the soft dirt at the base of the tree. Stares-at-moon skittered unceremoniously off his back. The long tail clambered up the exposed roots of the tree to find a perch on a low branch. It watched Heath digging determinedly below.

"That's an awful lot of effort when we could already be snug inside," it noted dryly, fluffing up its fur. Heath ignored it and continued to dig. The dirt under his paws gave way easily, disturbing small beetles that lurked there. It felt good to dig. He felt more like a rabbit. There had been so many un-rabbit-like thoughts in the last few days that he wasn't sure how he was supposed to think anymore.

We have to find the unicorn, he reminded himself, *then it will show us the way home.*

But a little voice, no more than a whisper in his thoughts asked, *but what if it doesn't?*

He brushed the voice aside and continued to dig.

Millet surveyed the area, stepping around the thicket and searching for any movement or sound. She jumped as a hidden cricket broke cover between her feet and bounced away into the grass. She bounded back to her brother, fur standing on edge.

"Didn't spot the little chirper, eh fluffy-butt?" Stares-at-moon chortled. "Pity, they're good eating."

"You eat them?" Millet asked, surprised, ears perked up as high as they would go.

"Oh yes," confessed Stares-at-moon. "When I can catch them. Fast little chirpers." Its long nimble fingers mimed holding a cricket as it pretended to tuck in greedily, long incisors flashing like blades.

"That's…that's awful," Millet gasped, recoiling slightly. "I thought you ate seeds, plants like us!"

"Oh I do," Stares-at-moon explained, "but I eat the chirpers too. Very filling. So are flutter-bys if I'm lucky. They fit well in my tummy."

"But...but..." Millet stammered. Heath stopping digging and sat to listen for a moment. He was sweating. Digging seemed more effort that he remembered.

"But they are alive!" She finally came up with.

"Yes," said Stares-at-moon, staring down at her from its perch, "and so am I. Why does that mean eating them is wrong?"

"Because they might feel," Millet insisted, sitting up on her haunches, trying to see eye to eye with the long tail. "Things often try to eat us and we don't like it. They might not either."

Stares-at-moon yawned. "I never hear them protest."

"Well you wouldn't if you're eating their head!" Stares-at-moon sighed and rolled its eyes, an impressive feat for a long tail.

"You're worrying too much," it muttered, leaning forward to look her in the eye. "It's really simple. I need to eat. Chirpers are good food. If I can catch them, I will eat them. Understand this; they are very good to eat."

"Yes, they are," said a deep, soft voice from a golden mouth that seemed to appear from the branch itself beside Stares-at-moon. The long tail squeaked with fright and fell forwards off the branch, landing on Millet. Heath stepped forward, ready to defend his sister, though the mouth didn't move. To Heath it looked like the golden mouth had appeared out of the branch itself. He saw two wide, brown eyes open either side of it, nestled in bark. The mouth shut, and he could barely see where it had been, but the eyes remained, staring at him. He perceived no difference between where the creature began and the tree ended. He couldn't be sure it wasn't part of the tree. After all, strange things had happened lately.

Stares-at-moon scrambled to untangle itself from Millet. Millet bolted behind Heath, staring at the talking branch. Stares-at-moon scampered behind her. The branch hadn't moved. The eyes continued to watch them. Pupils widened as it focused on the rabbits.

"What are you?" Heath finally asked. Large brown eyes blinked slowly and the branch trembled. The golden mouth opened, and now he was looking for it Heath realised it was more like a beak than a mouth, with a small triangular tongue. The whole broken branch turned to look down at the three of them. Pieces of bark shifted as it moved. Heath dared not blink. It lifted itself, and Heath saw feet appear, scaled toes tipped with wicked talons, like those of the hawk that raked him not so long ago. Wings unfurled either side from the branch, the same twisted grey of the bark, with paler streaks rippling through them. The whole branch seemed to bend as the creature moved to focus on them, shifting its weight.

"I am Leaf On The Wind," breathed the soft voice of the creature, swaying side to side though the eyes appeared to remain perfectly still.

"You're not a leaf," Millet remarked, slightly braver now death was not immediately apparent. Heath still felt uneasy about those talons. They were smaller than the hawk, but not small enough to satisfy his natural rabbit caution. The eyes widened. Its mouth opened impossibly huge, like that of a frog. The creature hissed as it breathed. Heath's heart was pumping furiously. His thoughts wanted to run. It sounded angry.

"I am Leaf On The Wind," it hissed again, stretching its talons one by one. The golden mouth gaped, then snapped shut with surprising force. The thud of the closing beak echoed in Heath's ears.

Suddenly it leapt with a great flap of its wings, gliding over Heath's head. It was so close he felt the air move around it as it brushed past him.

It was soft. He hadn't expected it to be soft.

A heartbeat later it had passed him and drifted out from under the tree, over the open grass. He hadn't heard a sound. Heath took a few steps after it, trying to see where it went. Millet was quickly beside him.

"What was that?" Heath wondered out loud.

"Maybe it was the dryad?" Millet suggested. "The book said they turn into trees." Heath considered this. The creature certainly had looked like the tree. If it had not spoken, he would never have known it was there. Judging by how close Stares-at-moon had been to it, the long tail hadn't known it was there either. It could have sat there, all night, watching them. He shivered. He took his gaze away from the direction the dryad had taken.

"Where is Stares-at-moon?" he asked. They looked around urgently, seeing no sign of the long tail. They hopped back to the tree, looking for any sign.

"Stares-at-moon?" Millet whispered. "Are you still here?" A different kind of fear surfaced in Heath's mind, not fear for himself, but fear for another life. He was sure he hadn't seen a tail dangling between those talons.

A familiar long nose cautiously peeked from the shallow burrow Heath had dug.

"Oh! You're okay!" Millet gushed, bounding up to it. The long tail emerged cautiously, shivering.

"Is it gone?"

"I think so," said Heath, still listening to their surroundings, even though he knew it may not help. "But how can we be sure?" Stares-at-moon crept out, hunched over and trying to keep small.

"Are you sure we can't sleep somewhere else?" it asked. Heath stared longingly at the burrow he had started to dig. He was running out of energy, and the burrow needed more work before it was fit to sleep in, and he just didn't have the strength to finish. Heath said nothing, but longed to feel the earth around him so badly. Millet watched him carefully with her concerned expression. It was becoming increasingly familiar.

"I'll dig," she said, and without another word went down the burrow, kicking out sprays of dirt as she worked. Heath watched in silence. Stares-at-moon crept up beside him, hunching down for protection in case the dryad returned.

"I don't think it will come underground," Heath said eventually.

"I hope for my sake you're right," Stares-at-moon muttered.

It was clinging to its own tail, fiddling with the tip nervously. Heath wondered if the creature's tiny ears heard as well as his did. Admittedly it hadn't made much difference with the other silent flying creature from their night in the mud.

"Fear not, long tail," Heath said, making himself stand taller and look stronger than he felt. "I have fought off bigger flying hunters than the dryad. The day we came through the stone burrow a hawk chased us with fire, and I fought it off then. I can do it again."

"That is good to know," replied Stares-at-moon, "but I do not yet feel safe here."

"If you had seen me fight the hawk, you would," Heath insisted. "It would dive into the fire while others ran, then emerge carrying flames in its talons. New fires sprung up wherever it landed until we were surrounded. It was fearless and clever. The fire never burnt it."

"What if your hawk is in fact a phoenix?" Stares-at-moon mused, scratching his chin. "For it is said that some creatures are not what they appear." The long tail paused, then looked Heath straight in the eye. "Tell me fluffy-butt, were the others afraid and confused?"

"Why yes, I believe so."

"Then why weren't you?"

"Oh, but I was," Heath insisted, "but I remembered how to think. My thoughts are strong."

"I see,' the long tail mused, though his tone made Heath wonder whether he truly did. "And why is that?"

Heath had to think for a few moments, though his thoughts

provided no answer. He settled for his usual response. "I don't know."

… And hardly ever what we dream.

When Millet had finished broadening the burrow, the three travellers made themselves comfortable in its depths. It was still much shallower than the burrows of home and lacked the familiar dry grass and fur which had been laid down over generations. Still, it felt better than the strange places they had slept the last few nights. The three of them curled up together. Millet and Heath slept nose to tail and Stares-at-moon curled up into a ball between them, wrapping itself in its long hairless tail. Heath listened as he dozed off, not only to the wind outside and his friends' soft breaths, but also to his thoughts. *Some creatures are not what they appear,* they repeated back to him in the long tail's words.

Well what are they supposed to be then? he wondered. *Can a bird be a tree and a hawk be a phoenix? What can a rabbit be if not a rabbit?*

Though the burrow was basic and shallow, Heath slept better than he had the last few nights. The sensation of dirt and fur provided some comfort even if it was not quite the dirt of home. Heath even dreamed.

He wandered through a white mist. There was no clear path, so he would stop and choose a new direction after a few steps. There was noise, an unending repetition of thumping on the ground he stood on. He felt the vibration in his feet. Two thumps, then a pause, then two thumps again, repeating over and over. It sounded like someone, or something, approaching hesitantly, as though unsure of the direction. Whatever the source of the noise, it sounded large. He took a few more steps through the mist. There was no dirt under his feet in which to leave tracks. Something grew like fine, grey-brown grass instead. It gave a little under his paws, but held no footprint.

The noise unsettled him, even in the dream. Heath kept moving, listening carefully, attempting to determine whether the noise was moving closer or further away. Somehow it always felt nearby and never changed in its rhythm.

I wonder if it's looking for me, Heath thought, *I wonder what it is.*

Do I wonder enough to find out?

Not yet certain of his bravery Heath continued to wander through the mist. He did not question how he came to be here, only considered what to do next. The grass beneath his feet became a little darker as he carried on, and he thought the noise grew slightly fainter. If something was looking for him, he was getting further away. Whether that was a good thing or not would remain to be seen.

The ground sloped upwards and Heath began to climb, increasingly bold. The concept of being lost hadn't even occurred to him.

It must be a big thing, making the noise, he thought. *It would have to be for me to feel its footsteps through my feet. Maybe it's the Great Stonecutter Rabbit. He might be looking for me. He might guide us home.*

Maybe the Stonecutter Rabbit is real.

The concept filled Heath's mind with equal parts hope and fear. If it was real, then it would surely know the way back, but would such a large creature care at all for their little needs?

The grey grass underfoot grew shorter here. He wandered on. Did he dare to find out which scenario would hold true for the Stonecutter Rabbit? What would he do with the answer once he had it?

A narrow stalk of some plant, devoid of leaves, became visible as Heath approached. Its bark was nearly black, its top vanishing into the swirling white mist. It swayed gently above him though it was so high its top vanished from sight. Heath sat next to it for a moment, stretched up on his hind legs before ultimately deciding to continue. He passed another of the tall narrow trees, and another and another on his haphazard journey. He never saw their tops, though the surrounding ground did not seem to grow any darker, such as it was in the mist.

The ground sloped downwards from either side of him, like a little ridge. He wandered down the lowest path, wondering at the simplicity of the landscape. No burrows, no tracks, no fallen leaves, just the same grey-brown grass.

He paused in his thoughts as something loomed ahead of him in the mist. It might have been a hill, but didn't seem quite so solid somehow. He watched for a moment, the endless thumping pattern softer under his feet, before continuing at a slower pace. For the moment at least, he seemed to be alone here.

The mound had an oddly reflective property as he approached. It was easily tall and broad enough to be a hill, he could probably climb it if he dared. He saw the white mist swirling on the other side of it, but not through it. The mist drifted over its surface as though made of water. He crept closer, noticing more of the narrow trees growing in a rim around the watery hill. He saw the tops of these trees. They were completely devoid of branches or leaves. Each grew to a narrow taper and leaned away from the watery hill.

Heath stared for a few breaths. The hill resembled water, clear and fresh with not a speck of anything else in it, yet it didn't flow. It remained perfectly still. The dome sat there like a drop of dew on a leaf of grass, only much too big to defy gravity for long.

He couldn't see what lay within it, so continued hopping slowly up to its edge. The curve of the hill distorted the ground below, but as Heath got closer he could just make out a rough, brown and gold surface underneath. Beyond it, under the centre of the watery hill, was a black hole. Heath saw nothing beyond that. He looked around at the surrounding rim of tapered leafless trees and the swirling white mist surrounding the watery hill. The thump-thump-pause was still palpable under his feet, but weaker than it had been.

He turned back to the watery hill and caught his reflection on its perfect surface. Upright ears, long twitching whiskers and wide brown eyes.

Just a rabbit. Nothing more.

He cocked his head, confused by the thought. *What more could I possibly need to be?*

Heath crept forward, sniffing his reflection. Of course there was no scent, he was the only one here. His whiskers brushed against the watery hill, rabbit met reflection, but the water did not give way.

Suddenly the ground below him trembled. The black hole beneath the watery hill widened, expanded towards the edge where he stood. Heath stumbled backwards in fear. The rim of tapering trees were lifted by the ground they grew on, sliding over the surface of the watery hill and meeting in the middle. Heath gazed up in alarm. Even with the two edges brought together, none of the leafless trees touched each other or tangled.

They stayed that way for only a moment before both sheets of grey grass covered ground slid back down the way they had come, lying peaceful and flat once more. There was no sign of any disturbance under foot. All was still once more, save for the thump-thump, thump-thump Heath could still feel underfoot. He looked around. Nothing was coming through the mist. Nothing was moving.

He looked at his reflection once more in the perfectly smooth, watery hill.

He blinked.

Health woke with a shiver. Millet and Stares-at-moon were no longer in the burrow. He was alone. He fluffed up his fur and crawled out of the burrow. The dawn felt colder than it should have for summer. Mist had settled on the open grassy paths between the scraggly trees, not unlike the mist from his dream. He could vaguely make out the hunched shape of Millet grazing on the grass edge, surveying the area with a mouth full of food. Stares-at-moon sat on a broken branch, peeling away chunks of bark and foraging for unlucky bugs in the crevices therein.

Heath hopped towards them in the dim light, but tripped over his own feet and landed heavily on his face.

Millet startled and spun around to face him. She bounded over to him as he tried to pick himself up.

"You're not alright," she told him flatly. "You're definitely not alright." Heath pulled himself shakily to his feet and shook himself. He stared at his sister. Her appearance was different. He couldn't see her whiskers and her eyes looked dull.

"Aren't I?" He tried to read her expression. It was probably concerned.

"No, you're not," she insisted. "You haven't been right for a while." Stares-at-moon scurried over.

"She's right, your eyes are swollen," it said, scrutinising Heath's face, "and your lips." Heath rubbed his paws on his face. His eyelids were a bit swollen, but his toes were numb. Millet sniffed his face closely and ran her nose across his long ears. She pulled back suddenly and sat upright, alert and on edge. She didn't say anything for what seemed like the longest time.

"I'm sure you'll be alright," she whispered.

"Are you sure?" remarked Stares-at-moon, "because he doesn't look-"

"Let's find the unicorn," Millet said firmly. "Now!"

Stares-at-moon no longer chose to ride on Heath's shoulders. Instead the long tail walked beside him, gently reminding him which direction they were going if he veered off track. Heath didn't even realise when he was doing it. All he tried to do was focus on the regular white flash of Millet's tail as she ranged ahead. His thoughts felt dull as though they were covered in the same fog that coated the world in the early morning.

Why did she hesitate? asked one thought. *She thinks you're going to die*, whispered another. *She should be getting as far away from your sickness as she can.*

But why lie then? insisted a different thought, *It's not in her interest.*

Why would a rabbit make itself a target for a hawk?

Some creatures are not what they appear, whispered the faintest thought. *What are we?*

Ahead of him Millet stopped in her tracks in the middle of an open patch of low grass. Heath and Stares-at-moon caught up to her slowly.

"Found something?" Stares-at-moon asked her, looking uneasy in the open even when flanked by the two rabbits.

"Do you know what this is?" she asked, nudging a dark brown pile with her paw. Heath squinted through his blurry vision. It smelled similar to their own scats, but was larger and moister, as though dozens of small pellets had been condensed together into the larger shape. *Perhaps it's the Stonecutter Rabbit,* he thought.

"Ah," said Stares-at-moon, running its nimble fingers over the pile of droppings with awe. "This, my fluffy-butted friends, is unicorn poo!"

Heath wasn't sure what all the excitement was about. Even if they could find the unicorn, they still had a long journey back, and he wasn't sure he'd be fit to travel. It all seemed a bit pointless.

"Are you sure?" Millet pressed. "Stares-at-moon, this is important."

"Of course I'm sure," the long tail assured her. "Why, it wasn't that long ago I saw a steaming pile just like this fall out of the unicorn's shiny white backside with my own two eyes!" The long tail sniffed the pile keenly.

"This can't be more than a day old," it said. "We can find it yet."

"Which way did it go?" Millet asked anxiously. "Can you tell?"

"Let's see what I can find," it said. Stares-at-moon skittered around in the short grass, sniffing and inspecting the ground. Millet watched with concern, spending equal time looking for danger, and looking at Heath.

"We'll find the unicorn," she told him after a while. "Stares-at-moon can find it, just like in the book."

"Then you'll find your way home," Heath whispered.

"Yes, *we* will." A small distance away, Stares-at-moon called to them.

"This way, fluffy-butts. We're off to find a unicorn!"

Stares-at-moon led them through the maze of grey stone and patchwork plants. Millet took up the middle ground, keeping one eye on the long tail as it wandered ahead of them, and coaxing Heath to keep up with them. Heath knew he was slowing them down, but part of him suspected it would be better that way. It would be easier for them to leave him behind. Millet, however, seemed to have other ideas.

"We need to rest," she decided, even though she still seemed fresh and full of energy. "Stares-at-moon, let's just stop for a few moments." Obligingly the long tail led them under a low bush. Heath was becoming aware of how little he had eaten in the last few days as the heat of the day grew harsher. The shade under the bush was littered with fine strands of yellow flowers that had fallen from the branches in recent days, though many more still hung there in round clusters.

"The unicorn is a big beast," Stares-at-moon warned them. "It can travel far in a day. We shouldn't rest long."

"Just a little while," Millet assured it, watching her brother lay down in the fallen petals and catch his breath. "We just need a little rest." The long tail shrugged and set about grooming itself. Heath felt weak all over, and his thoughts flew by erratically making it difficult to hold onto any single concept. Home, the warren, seemed so far away, and pointless to seek out. The darkness of the stone burrow, the flood of raging water and its chill rose to the surface of his mind as fever gripped him. He shivered, partly from illness and partly from memory. They had needed water so badly for so long, for so much of it to arrive at once seemed needlessly cruel. It was as though the sky had heard all their wishes for water and waited to grant them at the same time. The stone burrow had been terrifying, not knowing where they were going and being powerless to do anything about it. The weakness he felt now also made him powerless, yet somehow was not as frightening. He knew where sickness would ultimately take him. The absolute darkness had been so much worse. You couldn't run if you couldn't see, couldn't even try. Yes, the darkness was worse.

"The more of it there is, the less you see," Heath whispered. His companions pricked up their ears.

"What you say, fluffy-butt?" asked Stares-at-moon, creeping closer to hear better.

"The more there is, the less you see," Heath repeated. "It's darkness." The long tail clapped its hands together with glee. "Ah, very good fluffy-butt! You've got it! That's the riddle.

We'll make a thinker out of you yet!" Heath sighed and drifted back into his own thoughts.

Little birds chirped in the shrub above them. They were small things, covered in muted browns and no bigger than the small folk. Heath listened from his disjointed thoughts, but they had no words. He wondered for a moment why they didn't talk before it occurred to him in his addled state that perhaps the bigger question was why do any creatures talk in the first place.

"Yes, you mark my words, you long-eared fluffy-butted thing you," the long tail continued, "A great thinker you will be if you can puzzle through a riddle. A great thinker indeed. Won't all your other little fluffy-butts be impressed when you get home?" Heath's thoughts cleared a little as he struggled out of his daze. Would the other rabbits be impressed with riddles? They were profoundly impractical in communicating danger or food, and he was sure the Elders would declare them 'un-rabbit-like' if he tried to explain them.

"I doubt it," he muttered, sitting upright. "We should keep going. I'll be okay for a little while longer." Millet nodded.

"Tell me when you get tired," she insisted. "We'll stop whenever you need to."

"You shouldn't," Heath said, getting to his feet. "You should go on without the sick." Suddenly his sister was nose to nose with him, staring him down. Even though she was smaller, Heath backed away, dislodging the yellow petals stuck to his fur.

"Do not argue with me," she said sternly. "You're too sick.

Do as you're told." Heath flattened his ears are against his back and looked away. There was strength in her words, strength he didn't have. She would make a strong mother someday.

"Yes sister," he whispered, knowing to argue was futile.

The effort Heath needed to will himself forward seemed disproportionate to the distance they managed to travel. Every step felt heavy, and he constantly needed to remind himself which direction they were heading in. He would chat with States-at-moon to try to keep his mind focused on the here and now, rather than let his thoughts drift away into the fog behind his eyes.

There was certainly no fog in front of his eyes now. The heat had baked it away, but where the fog had left them, the blowflies had once again returned.

The flies had never shown any indication that they might speak, or even understand words. Heath wondered what might make them different, but his thoughts would not tie down any potential conclusion.

"Tell me more about the unicorn," he asked Stares-at-moon as they wandered across the short, tough grass. "What does it look like?"

"Huge," said Stares-at-moon, gesturing as best it could with its tiny fingers, clearly keen to tell a story. "And as white as it could be walking the dirt we live on. Its fur is thick and strong. It covers most of the beast's body, leaving only those black cloven feet sticking out the bottom. It's covered in twigs and leaves from its travels, and truth be told I didn't think it cleaned itself all that well."

"Why would you say that?" Heath wondered.

"Oh, the big beast had all manner of twigs and leaves stuck in its coat," Stares-at-moon continued. "Didn't look like it was able to reach them when it tried to scratch. Tried to get that big horn back there and dislodge them, but wasn't trying too hard. Probably tried to many times before, if you ask me. Which you did."

"Couldn't another one scratch it's back?" Heath wondered.

"Could do, could do," Stares-at-moon agreed. "But I've never seen any other but that one." Heath considered this while they walked, watching Millet ahead of them. *How lonely it must be to be the last,* he thought. *What lengths would one go to in order to not be alone?* They carried on in silence for a while, wandering from one tussock of grass to another, taking brief moments of refuge in the shade.

"Can the unicorn talk?" Heath asked out loud. "If it truly is the only one, who does it talk to?"

"Well I can't be so sure whether it talks," replied the long tail beside him. It looked around, in case anything might be listening to them before saying in a hushed whisper, "but I can guarantee the noble beast can curse like a wounded magpie!" Ahead of them, Millet waited by a vine growing over a crumbling stone barrier. She stayed there, more exposed than Heath thought she should be, until they caught up to her.

"Look at that." She gestured above them. Tangled in the vine's thorns, far beyond their reach, were broad tufts of thick white fur. They were stuck fast to the vine, but an enterprising small brown songbird was trying to dislodge a piece with fierce determination.

"Is it from the unicorn?" she asked, hope apparent in her voice. Stares-at-moon clambered up the vine. It placed its feet carefully to avoid the long thorns among its large leaves, once green but turning brown in the unrelenting summer. The long tail made its way painstakingly up the vine, eventually grabbing hold of a tuft of white fur in its mouth and carefully dragged it back down. The rabbits waited at the bottom, Millet with eager anticipation, Heath with bemused exhaustion.

"Well, is it?" Millet demanded, hopping back and forth, unable to hide her excitement.

"Ood oo ate a init," mumbled Stares-at-moon, carefully placing its feet on the way down. "Ashents uffy uts!" The long tail finally made it to the ground, removed the fur lodged firmly in its mouth and laid it out on the warm grey stone under their feet. The rabbits sniffed it curiously. Even with his muted senses Heath could detect the scent of flowers and green grass and the aroma of warm earth. Underneath them hid a peculiar musky odour which he assumed must be the noble beast itself. It was strange, but the familiar scents with it were oddly comforting.

"Definitely our unicorn," Stares-at-moon declared. "No mistaking it."

"Does that mean we're on the right track?" Millet asked hopefully.

"I dare say so." Above them more little songbirds gathered to steal away the tangled fur. "I dare say we're not too far behind." Millet bounced a little with a mix of joy and hope.

"That's wonderful!" she exclaimed.

"Brother, we'll find the unicorn soon! Really soon!" She bounced around him faster than his tired body could follow.

"The noble unicorn with its healing horn! It will fix you brother! I know it will!" Heath's brow furrowed. *So that was why she was so desperate to find it*, he realised, *she expects it to heal me. She thinks the stories are true. But what if they're not? What if the unicorn is no more real at the end of this journey than the Great Stonecutter Rabbit was at the end of the stone burrow?*

He kept these thoughts to himself, however, lacking both the energy and the motivation to question her conviction.

"Yes," he said flatly, not really believing it himself. She nuzzled his head worriedly, but at the same time suggesting she had faith everything would be alright.

"Yes," she agreed. "Are you still able to travel?"

"I could use a rest," he admitted, "and something to eat." He hadn't told her, but his guts felt heavy and painful. He knew he hadn't eaten well lately.

"I'll find a shady spot with sweet grass for you," offered Stares-at-moon, wiping the last strands of unicorn fur from its whiskers. The long tail scurried away around the edge of the vine covered stone barrier. A particularly bold songbird landed and hopped closer to them, eyeing off the discarded tuft of fur. Millet backed away from the fur, and the little bird speedily grabbed the tuft and fluttered away.

"We will get home," she told him, "Both of us. I know it. You'll see."

"I don't know these things as certainly as you do," Heath

admitted.

"You don't have to," she said, comfortingly. "You just have to hang on long enough to see them happen."

Suddenly a bloodcurdling shriek erupted from behind the vine. Heath's first instinct was to run away from the noise, but instead he found himself staggering towards it. Millet rounded the corner ahead of him, braked sharply and stared in shock.

Writhing on the ground in front of her was Stares-at-moon, clutching at its side and shrieking. Behind him, its long body half hidden by the undergrowth, lay a black serpent. Its neck and head rose off the ground, coiled for another strike. The black, glistening scales of its back concealed its small dark eyes, but its belly was bright orange, like the fire the rabbits had fled not so long ago. It reared back and hissed at the rabbits, revealing its long, forward facing fangs, dripping with venom.

Be cunning and full of tricks.

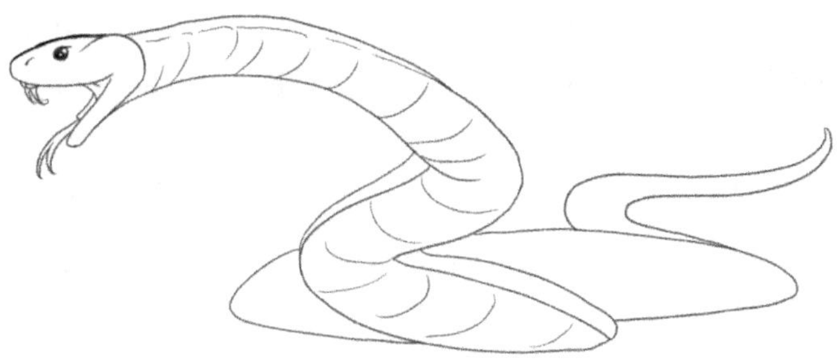

"It burns!" moaned Stares-at-moon. "Help me, it burns!" The serpent swayed from side to side, eyeing off each of the rabbits in turn.

"What have you done!" Millet screeched, her eyes wide with panic.

"It bit me!" Stares-at-moon cried, doubling over. "Oh it burns! It burns so much!" The long tail collapsed and lay on its side, panting. It stared up at the serpent that had struck it with wide eyes. Heath smelled the fear pouring off Stares-at-moon. The orange belly of the serpent almost glowed as it recoiled back into the shade of its hiding spot, but it did not flee. Neither did it try to strike either rabbit.

"I eats," hissed the serpent, a forked tongue flicking the air in front of it. No doubt it was trying to make sense of them as much as they were of it.

"No!" Millet spat back, thumping her foot on the ground. The serpent recoiled at her outburst. "No! Stares-at-moon, you'll be okay!" She hovered around the long tail, not turning her back on the serpent whilst as the same time wanting to inspect her bitten friend. Blood was oozing from the two puncture wounds on its side, staining its fur. Stares-at-moon gasped for breath, rolling over, chest heaving desperately for air.

"It burns," the long tail breathed. "It burns, so bright…" *Fire in its mouth and its belly,* Heath thought, *and a very long tail. Could it really be?*

Millet had grabbed Stares-at-moon's leg in her mouth and tried to drag the long tail away even as its breath gurgled weakly. The serpent hissed and lunged towards them, but did not strike. Millet jumped back out of the way.

"I know what you are," Heath said loudly, taking an unsteady step towards the swaying serpent. It hovered over its own coiled body, swaying its head side to side. The orange neck flared to appear even bigger as it hissed threateningly.

"So bright…" Stares-at-moon murmured.

"You're the dragon," Heath said. "You must be." The serpent

said nothing but continued to sway, eyeing off each of the rabbits and the dying long tail.

"Long of tail and the burning belly, fire in your mouth. You are the terrible dragon," Heath continued, unsure what compelled him. The serpent focused on him now, flicking the air with its forked tongue. It lowered its body to the ground, unnaturally flat. Beside him, Stares-at-moon's breathing became fast, wet and shallow. The long tail mumbled something in a raspy final breath. Millet crouched close to hear it, holding back her own whimpers as she tried to listen.

"Terrible dragon, it is said you may hold wisdom for us," Heath said. He swayed a little and felt woozy.

"It's dead," Millet moaned. "Heath, Stares-at-moon is dead." Heath ignored her for the moment.

"We're looking for the unicorn," he said to the serpent, or dragon, or whatever it was. "Tell us where it is."

"That thing is a monster," Millet cried. "It's a killer. Don't trust it!"

"Tell us what we want to know," Heath insisted.

"Sss… Why?" the dragon breathed. It lay almost motionless on the ground; Heath couldn't even see it breathing. The only motion was the regular flicking if its tongue and the dilation of its irises as it watched them.

"Because…" Heath stumbled over his own thoughts now. "Because you've slain our guide. You have to tell us where to go."

"…Why?" the dragon repeated. Its voice was soft and low, eerily devoid of emotion. Millet stepped back from Stares-at-moon's body.

"Because we need you to," Heath struggled. "Do you know where we can find it?" The dragon lifted its head slightly and nodded.

"Yes…"

"So you'll tell us where?" said Heath. The dragon hissed a few times in short succession. It almost sounded like laughing.

"No," it hissed. It lunged towards Heath, mouth gaping, fangs dripping with burning venom. Heath jumped back, tripping over his own feet, but felt no bite. Part of him wondered if the dragon had intended to strike him at all, or if it was only threatening. Millet hid behind him, trembling. With an angry hiss the dragon drew itself up high to look down on them. Both rabbits backed away, fearful. The dragon was huge, Heath couldn't be certain where its coiling black body ended. It glistened in the sun, rolling over itself, flashing its bright orange belly. It slid around Stares-at-moon's body, tasting the air around it. Reading any emotion on its scaly face was impossible though its intent was clear.

The rabbits watched in horror as dragon slithered behind Stares-at-moon's body, opened its maw and began to slowly, methodically engulf the long tail. It started at the haunches, the dragon's mouth opening impossibly wide as its lips slowly crept across the surface of their friend.

"How could it?" Millet cried. "How could it kill it? And then eat it?" The dragon's eyes remained fixed on the terrified rabbits while its lips worked away.

"Hassss to eats…" it murmured, its mouth full. The rabbits recoiled.

"But why us?" she cried. "Why not eat grass and seeds? Why must other creatures eat living things?" She turned on the feeding dragon. "Why do you have to kill?" she insisted.

"Needs to eat," mumbled the dragon, working its maw around Stares-at-moon. As sections of the long tail's body disappeared into the serpent, the creature seemed to expand in girth to accommodate its meal.

"But why living things?" Millet cried. "Why do you have to do it?" Grief-stricken she took a step forward. The dragon recoiled, dragging its meal firmly wedged in its mouth.

"You let it go!" Now she almost growled. "Let its body rest in peace." The dragon tried to drag his prize further away from the small angry rabbit.

"Can't," it mumbled around its meal, barely lifting a lip to let the sound out. "Ssshan't."

"Why not!" Millet protested, the loudest Heath had ever heard her be. She thumped her foot on the ground in anger. The dragon recoiled, pulling its meal over its twisting black body, either unwilling or unable to let go. Two thirds of Stares-at-moon still hung limply from its jaw.

"Let's go," Heath urged her. "We'll keep looking for the unicorn." He didn't like to see his sister so close to the dragon. The screams of Stares-at-moon still echoed in his hazy mind and he dreaded the thought of her being bitten. He couldn't bear it if she screamed like that.

"No!" she disagreed, not taking her eyes off the dragon, still trying to swallow its meal. Stares-at-moon's hind feet disappeared, sliding into its waiting throat. "We can't find it alone."

"We can't get Stares-at-moon back now," Heath pointed out, feeling woozy again, "and even if we could, what use would it be?" Millet said nothing, ignoring her brother and trying to stare down the dragon. Its head was much smaller than she was, but its long body was much, much larger. Heath hadn't believed it would try to swallow the long tail whole, let alone that it was doing so. He dared make no prediction whether it would succeed in swallowing a rabbit. He couldn't bear the thought of Millet sliding down into that fiery belly. The dragon's lips had reached the front legs of Stares-at-moon, already he was half gone. The pressure of its lips forced air out of the long tail's lungs, making Stares-at-moon's mouth gape and look like it was gasping. But the long tail was most certainly dead.

"Oh, you monster!" Millet eventually snapped, thumping her foot once more. Once again, the dragon drew back from the noise with a muffled, angry hiss.

"Don't make it angry," Heath urged her, stepping away. "Come on."

"No," Millet said, her tone as harsh and strong as the pale grey stone that was everywhere in this landscape. "No, no, no!" She thumped her hind leg against the ground, the universal rabbit warning noise for danger, again and again, as rapidly as she could manage. The dragon drew back, its mouth stuck firmly around its meal, trying to get away from the powerful noise vibrating through its body. Millet paused. The dragon relaxed and tried to slither away, trying to clear its mouth as quickly as possible.

Millet wouldn't let it. She dashed around to position herself in front of it and thumped a warning into the ground again. The dragon lashed out with its neck, slamming the ground nearby. She was too nimble for it and leaped easily out of the way, only to continue pounding the ground with her foot. The dragon curled tighter around itself, swinging its head side to side, looking for a way past her. The narrow face of Stares-at-moon drooped from between its scaled lips.

"You want me to stop?" she taunted the miserable creature. She paused in her thumping, one foot still raised threateningly, ready to fall, "then tell us how to find the unicorn. I know you can." The dragon twisted its head to glare directly at her, the front legs and head of Stares-at-moon dangling from its maw. Its beady eyes focused intently on her though Heath had no way to read its expression. Heath's only comfort was in knowing that while Stares-at-moon occupied its mouth, as much as he didn't want to think about it, the dragon was clearly not able to bite his sister.

"Tell me!" Millet demanded, thumping her foot once for emphasis. The dragon pulled its head backwards, flaring its neck to look larger, displaying the warm orange glow of its belly, so like the fire which had ultimately brought them here. It tried to hiss something around its mouthful, but Heath couldn't make out the words.

"Tell me and we'll leave," Millet promised it, her tone softening slightly. "Tell us how to find the unicorn." The dragon considered its options for a moment before slowly lowering its head back to the ground. Millet lowered her foot gently, waiting for it to speak. It lifted a lip to mumble something. Heath pricked up his ears to try to listen, but still couldn't hear it. Neither could Millet, he guessed, as she boldly took a step towards the dragon, head cocked to bring one ear closer. With bated breath Heath watched her approach it and the head slithered forward to meet her, the face and front feet of Stares-at-moon still protruding from its deadly maw. Heath felt queasy, weak and frightened. He wasn't sure how much of those feelings were due to the events in front of him, and how much was the sickness. Millet leaned over the dragon's head where it rested against the ground and lowered her ear to listen to its hissed whispers. Heath could not make out what was said, but saw her nod as she listened. While the dragon spoke to her it continued to swallow Stares-at-moon. The long tail's feet were gone now, only its lifeless head waited to disappear into the fiery belly of the beast. *We should be panicking,* he thought, *Rabbits should panic and run.* Yet he doubted he had the energy left to do so, and Millet seemed very far from panic.

"Thank you for your cooperation," Millet told the dragon matter-of-factly when she had finished listening. The dragon's mouth was nearly free, only a long, whiskered nose remained in it. Soon the fiery fangs would be free to strike once more. She hopped back to her brother, much calmer than any rabbit should have been.

"I know where to go now," she told him. "It's not very far." She nudged her brother back towards the open grass, away from the dragon. Behind them, the feeding dragon tried to slink away. Millet turned back towards it, considering her options as it slithered into the shadows. This was the last opportunity they would have before it was able to bite again. She turned away and set off after the unicorn.

Millet urged her brother to move quickly, but he needed little encouragement to leave the dragon's lair. He wasn't quite sure which direction they were going, and it seemed as though his sister often nudged him back onto one path or another. He was no longer watching the sky for danger, it took all his focus to simply watch where he placed his feet, and even they seemed to be blurry. His stomach growled for food, but his mind had no interest in finding any.

His little sister, soft, dainty Millet, how bold she had been to face down the dragon. She shouldn't have done that. Neither of them should have done that. Real, proper rabbits would have run and never looked back.

Some creatures are not what they appear, the words of Stares-at-moon echoed in his thoughts.

What are we then? he wondered. The words of Stares-at-moon didn't answer, and Heath did not wish to banish them from his thoughts. The words were all they had left of their friend.

"What did it say?" Heath murmured.

"What did who say?" Millet replied, not really focusing on Heath. She was ever vigilant, scanning their surroundings not just for danger, but for whatever she searched for. Her ears constantly twitched around, and she sniffed the air with purpose.

"Stares-at-moon. As it died, what did it say?"

"Oh," she said, still distracted. "It said 'go back to the books'."

Heath tried to determine why or even how the books could

help them now. They had already come so far, why would they go back? And in any case they couldn't read them.

"Is that where we're going?" he asked. He couldn't actually be sure which direction they were travelling in, only that his pace was slower than Millet would have liked.

"No," she told him softly, "We're going to find the unicorn. It sleeps in the purple forest. That is where we must go."

"How are you going to find it?" he wondered.

"The normal way," she replied, "No mystical tricks here, we just have to look for it." She urged him onwards, but every step he took felt heavier.

"I still need to rest," he told her, "I'm sorry, but I just can't keep going…" Millet sighed and looked at her brother critically. His eyes and lips were swollen, even his ears looked puffy, and his pace was so slow they might never find the purple forest.

"I'll find you some shade," she decided. "Come this way, just a little further." She guided him into an overgrown area in front of one of the many nearly identical stone structures. Low growing spindly bushes had taken hold between the thick, broad, inedible grasses growing there. She found some shade where the breeze would still reach him, for what little coolness it would bring. She cleared the twigs and leaves away so Heath could lie down with his belly on the cool dirt. He lay down gratefully and waited for his head to stop spinning. Millet scouted the area, satisfying herself that there way nothing but bugs around them, and a few small songbirds squabbling overhead.

"I'm going to leave you here," she whispered to her brother, "but I promise I'll come back. I'll find the unicorn, and it will help us." She nuzzled Heath's side like a worried mother doe. "You know the Elders don't approve of rabbits going places on their own," he reminded her. "They say it's not the cautious thing to do." She sighed at him in exasperation. "And what would the Elders say about long tails and facing down a dragon? Would they have any advice for dealing with a dryad or tracking down a unicorn? The world is bigger than the warren, and bigger than their experiences," she said. There was a new strength in his sister's voice that Heath had not heard before, or at least had never noticed. It was hard and stood firm like rock, whereas he had always thought of her as soft and giving like earth. *I suppose if you dig deep enough,* Heath thought, *you'll find stone somewhere.*

"I will find the unicorn," Millet insisted, "and it will help you. I promise." She bounded away a few paces, then thought better of it and quickly returned.

"Wait for me," she urged him. "Promise me." She waited for him to do so, but he couldn't find the strength for a promise he knew he may not be able to keep. After a lengthy silence, Millet left him under the shade, turning back to look at him only once more before seeking the unicorn on her own.

Heath lay on his side, lost in his own thoughts, for what felt like the longest time. His breathing was shallow and he barely moved, but still the fat, black blowflies found him here. They tried to steal moisture from his eyes though he could barely open his swollen eyelids. The wind brushed through the long grass and rustled the branches above him, but barely brought any coolness with it.

He was alone with his thoughts, and they were not peaceful company.

There were the physical thoughts, the ones that told him it was too hot, that he needed to drink and that there were flies bothering the wound in his hip. These thoughts were weak, distant and hard to listen to.

Then there were the proper rabbit thoughts, the ones the warren Elders would have approved of. They tried to quiet the other thoughts, tried to make him pay attention to the outside world, not the world inside his head.

Then there were the rest of them.

The un-rabbit-like thoughts, the ones the warren Elders never wanted to know, were vying for space and recognition. He had little choice but to listen to them now.

We should leave this place so Millet will not find us, said one thought. *Let her move on without us dragging her behind.*

But we promised, said another. *We promised to wait here while she finds the unicorn.*

And what if the unicorn isn't real, said the third thought. *There was no Stonecutter Rabbit at the end of the stone burrow, why should we believe there will be a unicorn waiting to show us the way home? Stories are wrong. They have done nothing for us but waste energy and time.*

The books told truths, said the second thought. *There was no Stonecutter Rabbit in the books.*

No, the third thought said, louder to be heard above the squabble of the others, *the creatures there are not real. The dryad was a bird, nothing more and nothing less. They're not real. Not real like rabbits are real.*

Some creatures are not what they appear, came a fourth thought that barely felt like his own. The words sounded like the sharp words of Stares-at-moon, but sounded far away. Heath tried to listen, to focus on them, but they were as insubstantial as the fog that danced behind his eyes.

The dragon was real, insisted the second un-rabbit-like thought. *Stares-at-moon knew it, and felt the burn. Tell the long tail its books were lies. Tell it that it felt no fire in the mouth of the dragon.*

Millet still has a chance without us, the first thought chimed up. *It will be kind of us to leave her now.*

No, the second thought insisted. *No, it will not be kind.* Heath thought he heard a thump in front of him. His eyes jolted open, as much as they could, and he stared at the blurry scene before him. He thought there was a rabbit standing in front of him, as pale and opalescent as the full moon, but only as substantial as a wisp of cloud. Its body seemed to give way and fade a little when the breeze blew over it, yet it remained standing in front of him. Heath thought he could see through it, to make out details of the long grass behind it, but still knew such a thing must be impossible. He struggled to sit up and focus on it better.

We must wait for her, must hold on like we promised, said the wisp of a rabbit, in the voice of his second thought. *She will come back for us.*

Not if she's got any sense, said another rabbit with the voice of the third thoughts. This rabbit was no more substantial than the first, but a darker grey, like the smoke of the fire brought by the hawk. Strands of dark grey would float upwards and away from its body though it never seemed to shrink in size. It had no eyes that Heath could see, only darker recesses in the smoke where they should have been. The white rabbit shook its head, dislodging more wisps of mist from its long ears that drifted away gently on the warn breeze.

Sense doesn't matter, it said. *Our sister has courage and strength.*

No, laughed the dark grey rabbit, though there was no mirth in its tone, *our little Millet is not strong. She is small and fragile and has always needed protecting.*

She has strength, insisted the white rabbit. *What else would she have, to face down a dragon?*

Lack of caution! A third rabbit appeared in the corner of Heath's vision, hopping towards the conversation. It sounded like a much older rabbit when it spoke, though its tone cracked when it grew louder. *It was foolishness alone to face down a dragon. No true rabbit would do such a thing!* Heath tried to look closer at the new rabbit. It seemed to grow more solid as he did so. It appeared gaunt, but furry, with eyes as black as the space between stars.

And who is to decide what is a real rabbit, wondered the white rabbit, bounding back into the centre of Heath's vision. *Are we not flesh and bone, born of does, born of does? Who is to decide who is a rabbit, and who is not?* The white rabbit sat in the centre of Heath's vision now, seeming less a wisp of mist and more like a real rabbit the longer he stared at it.

Some creatures are not what they appear, a new voice reached

Heath's ears, or a new thought rose to the front of his mind. Heath was no longer sure which. He looked around for it. Although it was familiar, it seemed out of place in the company of his own thoughts.

Waddling towards Heath and his thoughts, selecting the easiest path between the grass and the mists of his mind, came the translucent silhouette of the long tail, Stares-at-moon, dragging its spectral tail behind it.

Why must you always speak in riddles?

"How are you here?" Heath asked out loud. "You were eaten. You're dead."

Am I? What terrible news, said the shade of Shares-at-moon, grooming whiskers that were barely there. *A body can die, but thoughts and ideas live on. I'm a thought, an idea, nothing more or less, and I am one of yours.*

Why aren't you a rabbit, wondered the dark grey, smoky rabbit, circling the shade of Stares-at-moon cautiously.

Who says I'm not? demanded the shade, turning to the smoky rabbit.

Well just look at you, sneered the gaunt, old rabbit, looking the shade up and down. *A ridiculous, useless tail, pathetic little legs and no ears to speak of. You're no rabbit.*

Oh, but I thought a rabbit was not defined by his body alone, said the shade. It rose on its hind legs to draw eye to eye with the gaunt and smoky rabbits. *I thought a real rabbit was defined by proper rabbit thoughts?*

You are no proper rabbit thought, sneered the smoky rabbit, a hint of orange ember flaring in its recesses for eyes. *For you are clearly the thought of a long tail.*

Interesting, observed the shade of Stares-at-moon, sitting on its translucent haunches and inspecting its own ghostly tail with interest. *For here I am, clearly being thought by a rabbit. So where does that leave us I wonder?*

It leaves us sick and exposed under this useless bush, said the gaunt rabbit. Heath paid it little mind but continued to stare at the shade of Stares-at-moon. The other rabbits, his other thoughts, had grown more solid the more he looked at them. He wondered if Stares-at-moon could do the same. He wondered if he could somehow make it real. Strange things had happened in the last few days; he wouldn't be at all surprised at one more. Yet despite his staring, his focus, the shade became no more solid or real than it had been when it first waddled towards him. The shade acknowledged Heath's staring with no more than a twinkle where an eye should have been, like a fleeting glimpse of a star through cloud.

At least we've got each other, said the white, misty rabbit playfully. It licked its shimmering paws and washed its insubstantial face, as any normal rabbit would do, despite the fact that it was barely there.

Heath shook himself and tried to focus. His blowfly passengers dislodged themselves, but quickly settled again on his fur. None even tried to settle on the mystical rabbits which now kept him company. He wasn't sure why he had expected they would. He wasn't sure if it was a good thing that he could see his thoughts manifesting in front of him, nor if it would ultimately matter in any case.

Nothing will matter, came a new thought. *Not one bit of it.* Heath spun around to face the new thought, he was certain it had come from behind him. He looked for it, scanning the grass and the branches above, but he couldn't find the source.

You're going to die here and it will mean nothing, said the dark thought. It felt cold in the air, colder than Heath ever remembered anything feeling and left the acrid tang of blood in his mouth. He thought he saw movement, darkness, lurking in his peripheral vision and spun around once more, only to find his other rabbits sitting there, unmoved. The new voice filled him with dread.

"Where is it?" Heath asked. "Where's the dark voice?" The

rabbits of his mind in front of him tilted their heads as though they didn't truly understand the question.

It's behind you, the gaunt rabbit replied. Heath turned his head, trying to look behind himself. No matter where he looked the darkness did not shift from his periphery.

I'm always behind you, said the dark thoughts. *Always here.*

"What are you?" Heath asked anything that might be listening. "Show yourself!"

No, said the darkness, calm and taunting. *You can never face me. You can only carry me.* Heath crouched down, trying to look over his shoulder, trying to see the thoughts that lurked there.

Don't look at it, suggested the shade of Stares-at-moon, *looking only makes it stronger.*

Fight it, said the smoky rabbit. *We fought a hawk. We can fight this.*

But we were strong then, said the gaunt rabbit, faded to almost skeletal proportions. *We're not strong now.* Dread washed over Heath, and the darkness at the edge of his sight crept forward.

We're strong enough to still be standing here, the misty rabbit whispered. *Through all of it, we're still here.*

But for how long, wondered the dark thoughts. *Soon you will fall and be unable to rise. Soon I will have you.*

Dread gave way to panic.

Heath ran. He bolted forward, passing completely through the smoky rabbit as though it wasn't there. To be fair, it possibly wasn't.

He darted and stumbled between the tall grass, dodging in different directions, but the darkness always seemed to wait behind him.

Where will you run to, the dark thoughts taunted him, growing louder, stronger. Despite the heat of the sun, Heath felt its chill. *Where will you run to? Where will you fall and die?*

Panting now, Heath looked every which way, trying to find a path to take. The grass was shorter here, thick under foot, and the pale yellow brown of summer. He could no longer see the bushes Millet had hidden him under. He wasn't even sure which direction they were in, or how to get back.

There's no way back, said the dark thoughts, black tendrils creeping towards the centre of his vision. *You're lost. You're alone. You're sick.*

This is how rabbits die. Heath's legs buckled.

This is how you will die, the darkness whispered.

Here. Alone.

His eyes almost completely closed. He wanted to stop. He wanted to give up.

But there, in the centre of his vision, was a spark of yellow.

His nose twitched. It was a dandelion.

His thoughts drifted back to the small folk and their attempts to feed them, stuck at the bottom of the stone slopes. He remembered them chewing the ivy, and their singing.

The blackness slid back a little.

Twinkling eyes shone through. The shade of Stares-at-moon was there, sniffing the dandelion and watching him. The opalescent eyes of the white rabbit were there too, still gleaming, but its body was so faded Heath could hardly see where it began.

But they were there.

He focused on them now; their twinkling eyes and the dandelion. They stared back at him, waiting.

Some creatures are not what they seem, they said in unison, *but they may yet be what they dream.*

"Maybe I'm not a rabbit," Heath said our loud, challenging the darkness. "Maybe I'm something else."

What else would you possibly be, sneered the darkness, but it was already recoiling.

"Whatever I want to be," Heath told himself. "And I want to be alive!"

The shade of Stares-at-moon chuckled to itself. *Oh, don't we all,* it said to Heath, *but it takes so much more than just wanting.*

It takes willpower and fight in your heart, whispered the grey smoky rabbit beside him, barely more than a hint of itself remaining. *It takes anger, heat and action.*

"I want to be alive," Heath said again, trying to convince his own thoughts. The darkness drew back a little more, and he could see the other manifestations of his thoughts more clearly. He dared to hope.

The white rabbit became a little clearer in his mind's eye, a little more solid. A little more real.

It takes caution, and experience, said the gaunt rabbit, joining the other manifestations before him. Heath walked towards them very slowly, leaving the darkness behind him like a cloud. He sniffed the dandelion. It smelled like all dandelions had ever smelled, the one thing that had remained constant in all these strange days.

You will still fall, whispered the darkness, even as it grew fainter, *sooner or later you will still fall.*

But for now, we stand, thought the white rabbit. Heath stared at it as best he could, despite being woozy. Its white face was clearer now. It seemed to be covered in fur rather than mist and had the face of a young rabbit, not that unlike his own.

Without warning a shadow passed over Heath. He looked down to watch it glide silently by. It circled around him and he could make out the wings either side of it.

Two more joined it.

Run, hissed the gaunt rabbit, looking up at the sky. Heath looked up to see three birds circling him overhead. He knew the gaunt rabbit was right, he should run, but his legs simply didn't have the energy to do so.

"I can't," he mumbled, to himself more than any else.

Then think, whispered the shade of Stares-at-moon as it faded away. All his other thoughts faded as well, hopping back into his mind where they belonged. They left him as alone as he had ever been, staring up at the circling birds in the glaring sky.

His heart pounded in his chest and his mouth was dry. He didn't feel any better or stronger than he had a moment ago. It was fear alone that carved through the fog of his illness.

"Oh, ho, ho! Whatcha got down there!" He heard one of the birds say above him. He flattened himself against the brown grass, staring at the sky. It was too late to hope he hadn't been seen, but instincts took over anyway.

"Looks like we've got ourselves a little hopper. Silly thing!

Ha-ha-ha!" A bird landed beside him heavily on the grass. Heath jumped despite himself, but it made no move to attack him. It was not all that much bigger than Heath himself was. The bird looked at him sideways from twinkling dark brown eyes either side of a large, sturdy beak. It had wings of the same dark brown, but the body and most of its head was the pale colour of the dried, crumbling grass verging on white.

"You look lost, little hopper," it said. "Isn't that a funny thing?" This bird then erupted into laughter, flashing the pink inside of its sturdy beak. The other two birds landed nearby.

"Well no, I really don't think it is," Heath replied nervously. The other two birds were the same. Their talons we're smaller than the hawk, but Heath had no doubt they could do some damage if they tried. The tip of their beaks were hooked in a way no plant eater's ever were. If he had been fit and well he would have had no concerns defending himself or outrunning them. However, he was acutely aware that he was neither fit nor well.

"Hear that? He doesn't think it's funny!" squawked the second bird. Suddenly they all threw their heads back, beaks open, and cackled loudly at the sky.

"Guu-guu-guu-guu Barra-arra-arra-arra!" Their laughter echoed harshly in Heath's ears. It was so loud every creature in the world must know they were here.

"So, funny guy," said the first bird, peering at him with one eye, then swinging his beak around to peer at Heath with the other, "Tell us a joke. Whatcha doing out here alone? Where are your other hoppers?" Heath tried to calm down. After all, he hadn't been eaten yet.

"My home is far away," Heath said hesitantly, "But my sister is closer. She's looking for a unicorn." The third laughing bird cocked its head

"Why?" it asked simply.

"She thinks it will know our way home," Heath explained, "And that it will heal me. I'm very sick."

"Hear that? He's sick!" The birds erupted in a chorus of laughter once more. Heath didn't think it was that amusing, and their raucous chorus hurt his ears.

"Stop it!" Heath stamped his foot, but the birds paid no notice. "Leave me alone if you're going to be cruel." He tried to hop out of the centre of their circle, but they would teasingly step in front of him, wings outstretched, laughing all the while.

"If you're going somewhere," said one of the laughing birds, "You'd better… hop to it!" To which they all burst into noise once more.

"Guu-guu-guu-guu, Barra-arra-arra-arra!" Heath stared at them in confusion. Madness, that was it. The laughing birds had to be mad.

You're one to talk, thought one of the voices in his head.

"Oh! Oh! I've got one!" said the first laughing bird. "What do you call a little hopper that plays with foxes?" Heath didn't answer, he tried to hop through the gap between birds, but they fluttered around to block him, holding their mottled brown wings up. He was surrounded by feathers.

"Dinner!" squawked the second bird, resulting in another roar of their laughing calls. Heath wasn't sure what they wanted. They hadn't tried to eat him, but they also seemed unwilling to let him leave.

"I've got one! My turn!" cried the third bird. It hopped on the spot excitedly while the others starred at it, but always had one eye to swivel back to Heath. Heath gave up trying to escape them. He sat up on his haunches and picked up his ears to listen. If he couldn't run, at least he could try to think.

"How is a little hopper like a wattle flower?" the third bird asked. Heath thought for a moment. There were not a lot of ways he was like a wattle flower. He wasn't sure he understood the purpose of a joke, but it was starting to sound a bit like the riddle of Stares-at-moon.

"They're both fluffy!" suggested the first bird.

"Nope!" chuckled the third bird. It shuddered with the effort of containing its laughter.

"... We're not very tasty?" Heath suggested, figuring he didn't have much to lose in the circumstance. The birds all laughed their harsh, mocking laugh.

"Guu-guu-guu-guu, Barra-arra-arra-arra."

"That's not the answer!" mocked the third bird, clearly enjoying itself.

"Then what is it!" demanded the first bird.

"They're both yellow," the third bird snickered, barely able to contain itself, "Except for the hopper!" The ludicrous bird doubled over with its own laughter, flapping on its back with mirth. Heath drew back a little. That was far from a sensible answer, though it seemed to have great effect on the birds, who were still laughing enthusiastically. Heath had thought of himself as good with questions, perhaps that's what he needed now.

"I've got one," he offered tentatively, uncertain whether his riddle would be accepted, or even liked. The birds fell silent and focused intently upon him with their dark brown eyes, staring at him over their sturdy beaks. They remained motionless, staring at him in near silence. Heath felt queasy in his stomach, not all of it nerves.

"The more of it there is," Heath began, clutching at the tattered threads of bravery he had left, "the less you see. What is it?" He thought, just maybe, for the briefest moment, he saw the twinkle of the eyes of Stares-at-moon's shade appear behind the laughing birds. It was gone in a fleeting instant. Heath wondered whether he was going mad, but then reminded himself of the circumstance. He was far from home having survived a fire and a flood, a hawk, a dragon and a dryad. They had befriended the small folk and a long tail, moved books and understood riddles. If he had gone mad, it had happened some time ago.

"Guess," he urged the suddenly silent birds. They cocked their heads looking at each other and Heath in turn. They looked confused. Confused was better than angry.

"Sand?" croaked one, leaning closer to Heath, sounding unsure. Heath shook his head.

"Grass," suggested the second after looking around for inspiration.

"No," said Heath, growing increasingly confident in their uncertainty. The third bird flapped around in a circle for a moment, clearly struggling with the question.

"I know!" It declared proudly. "Eyelids! Haha haha!" It cackled at the sky, confident in its answer and clearly enjoying itself.

"No!" Heath yelled with all the strength he could muster, which admittedly was not as much as it should have been. "That's not the answer either." The birds stopped laughing at once and bounced towards him.

"Do you want me to tell you?" Heath asked, standing up to his full height, trying to convince himself as much as the birds that he really was as big and strong as he pretended to be. They waddled closer to him, their strong beaks mere centimeters from him. He smelled blood on their breath, still fresh, and he couldn't help but wonder what they must have eaten. He couldn't help but wonder whether they would have been this talkative if they hadn't already fed. They nodded in silent unison.

"Then I'll tell you," Heath offered, "but first I need you to do something for me." The laughing birds drew back, peering warily at the rabbit in their midst.

"Once you know the answer," Heath coaxed them, "you'll be the cleverest, funniest birds around." Apparently satisfied with this, the birds leaned closer again without a word, but with a new air of conspiracy.

"Find my sister," he told them. "Find her and the purple forest, and I'll tell you the answer." The mad birds looked at each other, wordlessly came to a decision and took to the sky.

Left alone in silence, Heath found that now even his thoughts wouldn't appear to keep him company. He headed towards the nearest trees for shade. The ground underneath his feet didn't quite feel solid. He thought that he swayed while he walked, but could do nothing to correct it. The trees had littered the ground beneath them with twigs, tiny oval leaves and tough seed pods. The canopy loomed high above him, but dozens of seedlings from the parent tree had taken root and provided some cover. He doubted it would keep him hidden from a determined predator, but the shade was welcome. The sun was high in the sky now, and he doubted he would cope waiting in the open. In any case, the birds were quite likely to find him wherever he hid. He wasn't sure it mattered in the end.

He flopped down among the roots of the trees, covering his white belly and tail, and fell into a deep sleep.

The first primroses were beginning to bloom.

The white fog was still present, but Heath had no sensation of walking anywhere, only floating. It was calming; the most peaceful Heath had ever been. He lacked a sense of up or down, or any direction. He could have easily stayed there forever, drifting slowly.

"Heath?" he heard Millet's voice from far away. "Brother, wake up." It was serene in the mist, but he still detected a desperate note in her distant voice. Her stress seemed so out of place as he floated, so jarring. He tried to wake, but didn't seem to go anywhere.

"Brother I need you," called her voice. "Wake up." He willed his legs to move, barely feeling them beneath him. The mist resisted his movements. It became thick, heavier than a moment ago, as though it didn't want to let him go. The peacefulness felt oppressive rather than soothing.

Heath began to panic. Maybe he wasn't resting here. Maybe he was trapped.

Suddenly he was falling through the mist, the wind rushing past his ears. The white turned to black.

He opened his eyes.

Millet's twitching nose occupied his entire field of vision, her whiskers brushing along his face.

"I'm awake," he mumbled and tried to right himself. She pulled back a step to let him rise on his own. He could barely make out the details of her face, even when he tried to focus. Somehow his sister looked less real than the figments of his thoughts had not so long ago.

"Brother, I found the purple forest," she whispered, "but there are some…uh…friends of yours?" She cast a worried glance behind her and the world erupted into noise.

"It's awake! It's awake!" chortled the mad birds before erupting once more into their jarring laughter. He could just make out the brown and white shapes a few paces away.

"Tell us!" they demanded, flapping over and hopping on the spot nearby. They kicked up leaves and twigs in their excitement, crushing a few of the smaller saplings that had struggled for light. He ignored them for a moment until he was certain he wasn't going to fall over. His head was spinning, and the sheer quantity of the birds' noise did not improve his concentration. He refused to look as sick as he felt.

"The more there is, the less you see," Heath stated, reminding them of the question. The mad laughing birds fell silent, waiting with bated breath. Heath was thankful for the silence, but knew it wouldn't last. Nevertheless, he held onto his words for as long as he dared before giving them the answer. What they would do once they had it was anybody's guess. For now they were his audience. They wanted the riddle, but he suspected from their talons and the scent on their breath that they were just as likely to want flesh. He hoped the riddle would be enough.

"It's darkness," he declared to the stunned silence of the birds. For a long moment, almost a lifetime in Heath's mind, they stared at him, stunned, their sturdy beaks gaping open. He smelled the acrid tones of blood on their breath once more, deeply unsettling to the proper rabbit thoughts in his brain.

Then one of the birds snapped its beak and started to laugh, softly at first, but growing in strength as it grappled with the concept.

"Darkness!" it cackled, throwing its head back in laughter. "Darkness! That's a good one!" the second bird began laughing with the first as all three took to the air, seeking perches on the lower branches above therm.

"Darkness eh? Can't see it well can you? Gu-gu-gu!"

"I still like eyelids," Heath heard the third bird complain as they disappeared higher into the trees.

"You would dumbo," the first bird replied, still laughing to itself. The rabbits watched them fly. Heath was thankful that seemed to be the end of it. He let out a relieved sigh.

"A love of riddles and a thirst for blood," Heath mused tiredly, "Are they the riddling sphinx?"

"Whatever they are, they're gone," Millet whispered. Heath nodded in recognition, struggling to form words. Why hadn't he stayed in the mist where it was restful and calm? Why had he come back to a world of effort and fatigue? He looked at his little sister.

It was because she'd asked him to. She didn't seem as small and delicate as she used to. He knew she hadn't grown much in the last few days, but the strength she carried was new. *Perhaps strength is something we learn,* he wondered.

"I found the purple forest," Millet told him excitedly as the laughter of the birds faded from his mind. "It's not as far away as I thought. We can make it."

"And the unicorn?" Heath asked. He hadn't really dared to hope, but Millet's excitement was catching.

"I haven't found it yet," Millet admitted though she did not appear at all dejected, "but I found some more scat. It must go there often." *This is it,* Heath thought, *one last journey to find out whether the books are true and whether the journey is worth it.*

Travelling was hard. Heath found himself no longer able to walk on his own and had to lean on his sister for support.

Even the blowflies bothering his wound and making it bleed afresh felt heavy. He was grateful that he no longer had to carry Stares-at-moon on his back, but then quickly felt a pang of guilt for thinking such a thought. The only reason he continued to struggle on was his sister's determination. Without her he would have stayed down long ago.

Heath paid barely any attention to his surroundings. He spent his energy watching his feet to avoid tripping, and tried not think about the likely future. Different coloured ground passed beneath his feet. Sometimes grass, but often the ubiquitous grey stone. Once or twice she led him across the hot black stone, and he thought they may have passed beneath the strange hunched piles that rested upon it. Millet seemed unconcerned by them now, and he was too tired to be afraid of anything. He wasn't sure where they were going, but Millet seemed to know. He trusted her. They travelled without speaking. It took so much effort to place his feet correctly and follow a straight line. How had he possibly spent his life so far walking and running with ease? Running was unimaginable now. If he fell again he doubted whether he would rise. He felt the shade as they walked through it, but never looked to see what it was from. He trusted his sister to look out for both of them, as unfair as that was on her.

"We're nearly there," she whispered in his ear. "A few more steps and then you can rest." Heath still did not raise his head. He could see the purple and white petals under his feet as he walked. He did not look up to see the plants from which they had fallen. The rabbits walked under the overgrown cover of a vast vine, its light green leaves freshly grown between the smothering expanses of draping purple flowers. Their scent hung heavy in the air like the flowers themselves. The vine covered every surface it could reach, including a nearby dead tree, and grew so many flowers that everything was drenched in purple.

Millet led Heath down the side of a long abandoned structure, another den of the They, also strangled by the irrepressible purple flowers. It felt like they walked through a burrow made out of purple petals, which was greatly preferable to the flooded stone burrow. The clearing beyond had short grass, clipped near to the ground by industrious teeth, with a myriad of small white flowers peeking through it. Heath was in no state to notice this either. White butterflies drifted between the heavily scented purple flowers, gorging themselves on the nectar within. A bright orange fish splashed at one that had drifted too close to the water's edge from a pool at the far side of the meadow. Tall, broad-leafed plants devoid of stems grew nearby with odd spiky flowers in orange and more purple, resembling the heads of birds. There were no songbirds singing here. The entire area was oddly quiet, save for the fish. Even the blowflies seemed to have wandered off, which was a small miracle in itself.

But there was no unicorn waiting in the meadow.

In his heart of hearts Heath hadn't really expected there to be one. The unicorn had sounded like a wish rather than a real creature of flesh and bone. Stares-at-moon had insisted it was real, but who knew how the long tail saw the world with its mismatched eyes? He felt Millet's disappointment as he leaned on her, she sagged slightly as she looked around.

"Come rest by the water," she told him, refusing to let her disappointment show in her voice. Not that it mattered much, Heath already understood what condition he was in. Millet guided him to a shady spot by the pond where the breeze was cool and soothing. He curled up on the short grass and shut his puffy eyelids. His whole face felt swollen, eyelids, lips and ears. Any part of him that didn't feel swollen felt numb. At least this would be a peaceful place to rest. He could rest here forever.

It was his sister he actually felt sorry for. She had tried so hard, and this would be where her efforts ended. Soon she would be on her own and need to face the long journey home with nobody to watch her back. It may yet prove an impossible task for her, despite the strength she had shown today. Even if she did make it home, would anyone believe her story? Would they acknowledge what she had faced, or dismiss it as fantasy? Would she ever be believed?

"Thank-you," he breathed. He could not muster much volume, but in this serene place not much was needed. The ripples on the pond's surface faded to stillness once more.

"You wait," Millet told him. "The unicorn will come back. You wait and see."

Heath let his eyes close and simply listened. He didn't have any energy left to spare. The meadow was oddly quiet. The butterflies made no noise as they hovered from plant to plant, and the orange fish was silent below the surface of the water. He could feel a soothing breeze blow across his fur, but he could barely hear the rustle of the broad-leafed plants or the surrounding purple vine.

It had never been truly quiet in the warren. There had always been other rabbits and their noise. The burrows were filled with footsteps, heartbeats and the occasional squeak of playing kits. Outside the leaves of the Great Eucalypt had always been noisy in the wind. Even when all other movement in the world had stopped he would hear the ever present buzz of the fat, lazy blowflies that always seemed to find him.

But not here. There were no flies here, and so little noise. Soon his own thoughts would come forward again, but he didn't want to hear them, not while Millet was still here.

"You should eat," he reminded his sister. "You're going to have a long journey ahead of you."

"Yes," she replied. "*We* are." He heard her fur rustle as she picked up her ears, listening intently. The meadow might possibly be the quietest place Heath had ever heard. *Or maybe my hearing is failing.* Eventually Millet hopped forward to the still pool. She lapped greedily at the water's edge. It was a good sound, and he wished he could join her. Either that, or to cease lingering, so that she could get on with her journey. There was little point in struggling. He couldn't run from sickness like the fire or fight it like the hawk. He certainly couldn't reason with it like the mad birds, if it even was reason that applied in their minds. All he could do was accept it, as much as that left a sour taste in his mouth. Or perhaps the taste was more of the sickness. However the disease had come across him he was glad that Millet seemed unaffected by it. It was another small blessing in this purple forest.

His mind was quiet now, though he sensed his many

thoughts were still there. Perhaps they were watching over him, and he would see them again if he dared to open his eyes, but he didn't care. Perhaps they knew he didn't want them now, and were patiently waiting their turn. He wondered if the dark thoughts were waiting for him too, and shivered at the thought.

"Sister," he breathed. Millet stood up from the pool, ears pricked towards him.

"Yes?" She hopped towards him to hear his trembling voice better.

"When you get home, don't let them tell you what to think," he told her. "The world is bigger than they know, and stranger than they ever imagined. No stories, none since the dust fell, would have prepared any of them for this place. It is only the thoughts, the ones they disapproved of, that have carried us this far." He stopped for a breath. Even talking was harder than it should have been. It didn't matter, soon he wouldn't have to do that either.

"Don't let them tell you what to think. Don't let them tell you this never happened. Tell them… Tell them new stories," he finished with a sigh.

"Brother?" Heath didn't respond. Millet leaned closer to him, nudging his chin with her nose.

"Brother?" she asked again, more urgency in her voice. He still did not respond.

If you are human enough to cry no
magic in the world can change you
back.

"Please," she whispered, barely audible. "Please speak to me."
Heath's breathing was slow and shallow. She could sense the
weak breaths on her whiskers, but only just. His eyelids and

lips were swollen. Even his long ears seemed puffy and out of proportion. The wound on his hip had crusted over with black scabs, but opened again during their journey. Not for the first time she wondered what would have happened if she had sought water at the stone burrow on her own. She could hardly see Heath's chest move now. She had never seen a rabbit die before. She had seen, or heard, them killed of course. Deaths at the warren had been quick and violent, bodies snatched away to feed the hungry predator that craved them. She knew what to do in those situations; run like the wind. But here, with the sickness and fading brother before her, there was nothing to run from. Nothing she knew how to do.

"Please," she begged her brother, "I don't want you to leave." Nothing to run from and an invisible foe to face. Some rabbits at the warren would claim that every death had a purpose, that there was a reason for the loss they must endure. Knowing others thought this offered Millet no comfort. Besides, she could see no reason why disease should take her brother from her. They had tried so hard, how could there possibly be a reason? How could this be fair? She felt the fear and sorrow well up within her, spreading through the core of her being like a bruise. It filled her, and she had no idea what to do with these feelings.

"I'll miss you," she whispered.

Then she did something that no rabbit since the stories were first told had ever done before.

She wept.

Small, precious tears dripped down her face, soaking her soft brown fur with moisture. She sobbed quietly, head bowed over her brother. She cried for her loss, and for her brother's loss of years, for the fear of being suddenly alone in the world, and for sorrow in its purest form. She wept with all her heart. She froze.

There was a noise behind her.

She spun around, ready for action, her vision still blurred by tears. She scanned her surroundings, seeking any kind of bolt hole or hiding place, yet her legs did not move. She could not will herself away from her brother. Something hardened in her heart and cleared her mind. If he couldn't run, she wouldn't either. She stopped weeping.

She would stay. Until the end of the earth, she would stay. There was no force, no creature that would move her little body from where she stood right now.

Just let them try.

Something was coming through the purple drenched corridor that the rabbits had hopped down not so long ago. It sounded large, Millet could hear the rustle of plants as it pushed through them and petals falling to the ground. She could hear the steady pace of its feet. Her body felt warm with a flush of anger. How dare something come into this place now, with her brother like this? She wasn't ready. It wasn't fair.

She tensed her body as she heard the creature approaching the corner. She wouldn't run away. She would face this thing and show the world what one little rabbit was made of. Flesh and blood, sorrow and fury. She was ready to take on the world, whatever the consequences might be. She was ready, and she was angry.

A creature pushed its way through the draping purple flowers of the vine. The plant bent and creaked as it rounded the corner. The creature was huge, easily a dozen times bigger than she was, maybe more. Even if she had intended to, she doubted she could have outrun it. She had no idea how she was going to defend her brother, but the heat and anger she felt welling up inside her was going to come out somehow. It was so unfair. They hadn't asked for this, for any of it. She had already lost one friend today, with nothing she could do about it. Nothing was going to make her move from this spot now, and there was no way she would allow something to eat her brother. Not today. Not while there was anything she could still do. She took a deep breath…

…and looked up into the face of the unicorn.

The unicorn lived in a lilac wood, and
she lived all alone.

Millet stared at the creature which had entered the meadow, heart pounding in her chest. Her jaw hung open in surprise.

The unicorn was bigger than she had expected it to be, easily a dozen, possibly two dozen, times taller than she was. It placed its black, two toed feet delicately to avoid crushing flowers underfoot. It was as white as Stares-at-moon had said and covered in a thick coat of shaggy fur. Twigs, leaves and flowers had become tangled in the matted fleece, making it seem as though the forest itself followed the creature as it walked. The eyes were golden and intelligent with broad pupils. A single great horn curved away from one side of its head, drifting away from its skull at right angles with a gentle wave.

The unicorn.

It gazed around the meadow placidly before wandering over to the flowering vine and grabbing a mouthful of new green leaves. It fed delicately, apparently unaware of the presence of the rabbits. Millet plucked up her courage, not even considering the possibility that she should be afraid.

"Excuse me!" she called to the unicorn. "Excuse me!" The unicorn looked around, still chewing its mouthful of leaves, before eventually looking down for the source of the noise in its serene meadow. It lowered its head, still chewing, to bring its eyes level with Millet. Millet dashed over, barely keeping her excitement and urgency in check.

"Please unicorn," she begged. "I've heard so much about you. We need your help."

"We?" asked the unicorn, its voice soft but raspy. It regarded her closely with one ancient golden eye.

"My brother," Millet explained. "He's very sick," she darted back to Heath, still lying by the pond.

"Brother wake up! The unicorn is here," she nudged him firmly, but he didn't stir. The unicorn, unconcerned by Millet's urgency, calmly wandered over to the pond. It sniffed the still body.

"What are you hoping I will do?" the unicorn asked.

"Heal him!" Millet begged, not even trying to hide her desperation. "That's what the books said you can do! Please! You're our only hope! You're his only hope…" The unicorn sniffed Heath from nose to tail and gave him a gentle nudge. Heath did not respond.

"I cannot," said the unicorn. It lifted its head and turned to walk away. It took short steps as though restricted or weighed down by the dense mats of fur and clumps of forest it carried with it. The creature was oddly beautiful despite the mass of plants tangled within its fleece.

"What do you mean you cannot?" Millet demanded, more shocked than angry. She ran after the unicorn, dashing between its legs to come up in front of it once more.

"You have to help him!" she insisted. "I know you can. Please!" The unicorn sighed, its breath smelled of crushed grass and leaves.

"You're very confident about a fact that simply isn't true," it told her, brushing her aside and casually picking a mouthful of clover.

"What do you mean it isn't true?" Millet whimpered, wide-eyed with a fear for her brother. The unicorn stared down its long nose at her and sighed, dropping fragments of crushed clover as it did so. Its breath was sweet, but its voice weary.

"I'm old and have walked these streets for many years," the

unicorn said softly, "I lived before the dust fell. I watched it rain down and coat every surface under the sky, saw its lights dance in every colour. I have seen the world both before and after the dust, in times when They walked with us, and now when They do not." Millet sat down to listen, not completely sure what she was hearing, or what this would have to do with Heath. Elders had spoken of old stories, told by their Elders and their Elders before them, about the dust falling and rabbits asking questions. The stories were generations old, from so long ago, yet here stood a creature who had lived to see them take place. *Perhaps unicorns don't die,* she thought.

"But you must be able to," Millet insisted. "You're the white creature with one horn. You've got two toes on each foot. I don't know what your tail is supposed to look like but I'm sure it's like a lion. You're a unicorn. You have a magic horn! You can help us. You can help my brother."

"Being very old and having walked very far grants me experience, not magical healing powers," the unicorn continued. "I am no more magical than you are, and no less." Millet thought desperately for a moment.

"What if you can, but you don't know it yet," she suggested, "Maybe you just have to try and see if he gets better?" The unicorn snorted, blowing back the fur of Millet's face, and pawed the ground with one cloven hoof.

"Do you honestly think in all my years I have never wished someone better?" it demanded, insulted. It shook itself and turned on the spot, carefully laying itself down among the grass and flowers.

"Let me tell you, bold one, what you do not know of the

world." Millet hopped closer to its head to listen, glancing worriedly at the limp body of her brother. Now comfortable, the unicorn gulped and regurgitated a mouth full of food to chew. Millet stared in shock.

"Before the dust fell, They were everywhere. They built these places and so much more. They fed us and sheltered us, clipped our fleece and cared for us. Sometimes they did strange and unknowable things, but for the most part things were simple."

"What did They want?" Millet asked.

"As far as I remember," the unicorn spoke as it chewed, "They wanted to watch us eat and pat our heads. They didn't have much fur, except on their own heads, so I assumed that's why they were obsessed with always touching ours. Especially their little ones." It paused and swallowed its mouthful of cud. "When the dust danced across the sky and fell upon us, we didn't understand. How could we? We'd not even wondered about stars. We carried on as normal, grazing our pasture. It was several days later as the grass grew thin and the water ran dry before we realised something was different." The unicorn sighed and rubbed the hornless side of its head against the ground.

"They used to care for all manner of creatures. Big gallopers, little yappers, frightening howlers, cunning hunters. Such variety of beasts I've not seen since, all because they wanted to pat our heads and stroke our fur." The unicorn paused and looked up at the darkening sky. Dusk was falling, and the heat of the day creeping away.

"There were even little creatures like yourself, in different colours. We used to live in a pen where they would pet us." The unicorn trailed off into her memories. Millet's ears pricked up to listen closer, intrigued. She hoped Heath was still listening, somehow.

"Of course, they weren't nearly as bold as you are," the unicorn told her. "We were penned in by a flimsy fence. It didn't take much for us to break through it. Others were not so fortunate." The unicorn stared at the abandoned structure on one side of the meadow. Its angular entrances were softened considerably by the intrusive purple vine, but it was still sturdy after many years.

"Some poor souls were kept in those," the unicorn said, a touch of regret in her voice. "Wherever They went, they left so quickly that they didn't open any gates. Left them locked inside, unable to open their ways out." *Trapped*, Millet thought, *trapped in those things with the books.*

"What happened to them?" Millet asked. "The creatures trapped inside."

"We tried," the unicorn confessed, "We broke holes in many of those things. Some were just too solid for us. We were only flesh and bone." The unicorn stopped sky gazing and turned back to the little rabbit beside her.

"I broke a horn, trying to batter my way into one of those things. I was trying to get them out. They had no food and little water. They didn't last long if we failed to free them. I would listen to them cry out for their masters, their providers, for anyone at all who would help them. They begged, and if they couldn't get out, then they died." Millet listened in shock to the unicorn's tale. Stares-at-moon had said there were dead things all over the place, but she hadn't imagined this would be the reason. Had Stares-at-moon known?

"Those structures," the unicorn gestured to the structure across the little meadow, "They were homes, once. They're tombs now." Millet shuddered. The chamber Stares-at-moon had read the books in had no scent of death, but how long ago would it have been? They hadn't explored the rest of the chambers. Had there been a skeleton nearby when they slept? Why had they not smelt it?

Millet's hairs stood up on end as she remembered Stares-at-moon wanting to eat the cricket. He'd been evasive about the bones in the buildings. How many small folk would it take to eat a corpse? Shivering, she looked around.

There were dozens… no, hundreds of tiny twinkling eyes peering out from the purple flowering vine on all sides, a swarm of the small folk hidden in the leaves.

"When did they get here?" Millet gasped. She hadn't heard a sound.

With a note of dread she had to wonder whether they had followed them the whole time.

"Oh?" The unicorn glanced around, unperturbed by the apparently sudden appearance of the small folk. "They often come by. They never make a peep." The unicorn's assurances didn't make her feel any better.

"They helped us once," Millet said, partly to reassure herself that they weren't dangerous, even though she didn't know exactly what they were anymore.

"Did they now? Their kind did well in the days after They left." The unicorn yawned and gulped another mouthful of cud into its mouth. "Others did not do so well. We were so used to our food being brought to us, many of us didn't know how to find it. The small folk did very well. They ate so much and got into so many places. Others…" The unicorn's voice trailed off.

"Others?" Millet prompted it. She needed to understand. If the unicorn couldn't or wouldn't help Heath, at least it could answer some of the questions he would have asked.

"The meat-eaters," the unicorn whispered, and Millet wondered if she detected a hint of fear from the mighty creature. "The cunning hunters would mostly eat the small folk, for there was always more of those, but the big howlers, well, the small folk are barely a mouthful for them. They wanted something more substantial, something bigger." The unicorn snorted in anger, not even looking at Millet as it relived the memory.

"To think we had freed most of them from their pens, from their tombs. We helped them, but it didn't matter. They wanted food, they hungered for flesh. Once they had the scent of it they were in a frenzy. It didn't matter what they took, who they ate. My kids," the unicorn paused, clearly having difficulty continuing, "… my sweet kids only screamed for a moment before their little voices were cut off, forever. Their mangled bodies haunt me. This entire place, this place that They build, is haunted for me." The unicorn sighed sadly and stared Millet firmly in the eye.

"If I could heal, if I could save, don't you think I would have saved them? Don't you think I would have tried my hardest? They are lost to me, and now I am the last." Millet sat in relative silence as she considered the unicorn's tale. She glanced at her brother lying motionless by the pond. She also felt like the last.

"You were a mother?" Millet asked in awe. She tried to imagine baby unicorns prancing in the meadow, playing like the kits back home.

"Was," the unicorn confirmed. "Now I only nurture these memories."

"Then why do you come back?" she asked at last. "If these places are so haunted to you, why so you come back? How can you face it?"

"I come so I don't forget," explained the unicorn, "and because I like to see the Fey."

"What's the Fey?" Millet asked. It didn't seem to matter how many answers she found, there were always more questions.

"Fey are like They were, but not quite the same. Fake. Fake They, the Fey. But they remind me of the days before the dust fell." The unicorn swallowed the cud she had been chewing.

"Back in those days They would cut this coat of fur from me, freeing me from it every Summer so that I could run and frolic. Now it weighs me down, slows me down. It's drenched and heavy in winter, stiflingly hot in summer. I shall not be able to carry its burden much longer. All I can do now is remember." *How terrible it must be to be weighed down by your own fur,* thought Millet. She shivered. It seemed so unfair that the days would bring such heat and yet the nights would still be so cold. She pawed at the matted fleece and entwined plants along the unicorn's flank. Her fur was dense and hopelessly tangled, covering her body like an impenetrable shell, but the fibres were soft and fine.

"Perhaps I can loosen it?" Millet offered, inspecting the mess of fur. If the unicorn truly couldn't help Heath, perhaps some good could still be done. Besides, she would be grateful to have a task to occupy her mind.

"You?" The unicorn laughed. "Little you? It would take you many cycles of the moon, though you are welcome to try." Millet pawed at the fur around the unicorn's foot, the fur was shorter and coarser here so easier to get a hold. She worked her way through it, nibbling away fine strands, until she pulled away a mouthful of the white fur. The unicorn chuckled at her and set about chewing its cud further. Millet carried the mouthful of fur over to her brother. It was impossible to see if he was still breathing, but it didn't matter. She tucked the mouthful of fur around him like a mother doe lining her nest. She wasn't going to let him get cold.

"I told you its real," she whispered, not expecting a reply. She returned to the unicorn to work free another mouthful of fur, then another. The unicorn didn't object, merely watched her placidly as it chewed.

"I have not seen your kind in these parts for some years," it said eventually as Millet continued to work. "How did you arrive in this place?" Millet dropped the tuft she had been working on to speak.

"My brother and I came from far away, but it was by accident," she explained. "There wasn't much water near our warren. I was very thirsty. He went with me to drink at the great stone burrow." She paused, sadness flooding her memory. "Then they sky lit up and struck the tree that grew over our warren. Everything was burning. We were separated from everyone else. When the rain finally fell, we were washed through the stone burrow, and came up in this place." Millet paused for breath, the unicorn waiting patiently, chewing all the while. "The small folk and a long tail helped us get out. The long tail said you might know the way back to our home. Then Heath fell sick…" Her voice trailed off as she found herself unable to speak further. Rather than sit in sadness, she chose to keep chewing at the unicorn's coat.

"When was this?" the unicorn asked softly.

"Two, wait, three days ago," Millet replied, trying to focus on the task in front of her and not the events that had brought them both here.

"It's all my fault," Millet whimpered. "If it wasn't for me, neither of us would be here now."

"Your fault?" marvelled the unicorn, its voice dripping with sarcasm. "So it was you that called light from the sky and started the fire. You who called the clouds to open and pour forth with rain. All your fault! Ha! And you believe I'm the magical creature!" Millet crouched down and flattened her ears. She wanted to be small and hidden, wanted to disappear. "Small one, it will be your fault the day you control the sky. I did see the storm front a few days past. I believe I know the path you must take to get home." The unicorn glanced knowingly at Heath's motionless body, gradually being covered in its own fur. "That is if you still wish to return." Millet shook herself back to the task at hand. She'd never seriously considered not returning and she'd always presumed Heath would be by her side.

"Where would I go?" Millet wondered, looking up into the unicorn's big golden eyes.

"You could stay here," the unicorn offered. "Keep me company, tell stories, see the Fey."

Heath would have wanted her to go home, she realised, and she wasn't prepared to stay on her own like the last of her kind. The unicorn was alone, and she could almost taste the sadness in the air when she spoke. Millet didn't want to end up like her. She knew she would long for other rabbits.

"I will try to go home," Millet decided, tugging more tufts of fur with her paws. "I don't want to be the last rabbit I ever see." The unicorn released a small burp of gas, smelling strongly of wet grass and not altogether unpleasant.

"Then I shall show you the way, when you are ready," the unicorn replied. "I appreciate you trying to help me out of my fur even if such a task is endless." Millet dragged another clump of white fur over to her brother and nudged it underneath him. She had built up a soft padded mat of it for him to lie on. He looked quite peaceful, but she dared not check him for breathing. She would rather not know.

"You have a visitor," the unicorn whispered. Millet hopped back to the front of the unicorn, not seeing anyone else present at first.

"Down there," the unicorn gestured beside her with her long white face.

A tiny, brown small folk sat there, waving a dandelion flower. It offered her the bright yellow bloom. Millet cocked her head to one side. It was impossible for her to tell whether this was the same individual that had thrown them the dandelion flower at the stone banks not so long ago. They had travelled quite far, surely little legs like those would be unable to keep up, but if it was a different small folk then how would it know? It held the flower out to her with its little paw, waiting for her to take it.

She hesitated at first, then decided of all the things she had been fearful of lately, this was by far the least deserving.

"Thank-you," she told it, "and, um, thank you or your friends when they've helped us before." She gently took the dandelion in her teeth. The small folk squeaked in apparent delight. Millet sat, holding the flower. She didn't really feel like eating, but wasn't certain what the small folk would think of her if she didn't. Dozens of their tiny faces watched her from the undergrowth, waiting for something.

She turned around and decided to take the dandelion back to her brother. They always were his favorite. She hopped over to where Heath lay, clumps of white fur tucked underneath him. Softly she lay the dandelion by his nose.

She thought she saw his nose twitch, but didn't dare entertain the possibility that she may have imagined it.

He looked peaceful resting on the bed of unicorn fur with his dandelion. Calm and free from fear. Millet turned away quickly, finding it too difficult to look at her brother for long. She sighed and hopped back to the waiting unicorn.

"They seem to have taken a bit of a shine to you," the unicorn noted. Millet looked behind her. A dozen small folk sat in the grass, watching her intently. They barely blinked. She tilted her head to one side, pondering what they wanted.

They mirrored her, tilting their heads the same way.

Millet straightened up and lifted a front paw as she leaned backwards, subconsciously preparing to run. The small folk did the same. She put her foot down, mimicked again.

"What do you want from me?" Millet asked them. They didn't answer her with words, but burst into a single note of song. She realised it wasn't just the dozen small folk sitting in front of her, but those in the vines surrounding them as well. Every single one had responded.

"They're very good, aren't they," the unicorn chuckled to herself. Millet stood up straight and puffed out her chest. She tried to make herself look like the biggest rabbit she could be.

"Well, if you're going to sit there staring you might as well make yourselves useful," she decided. Determined, but not quite sure why, she turned to the unicorn.

"Please sit still," she asked her. The creature tilted its head, the twisted horn almost touching the ground.

"Why?" she asked.

"I think they want to help," said Millet, with a little less confidence than she'd expected of herself. "We're about to find out." The little rabbit took a few tentative steps towards the unicorn. She didn't hear any noise from behind her, but didn't dare look back. She hopped back to the headway she had been making in the unicorn's coat, tiny though it had been, and busied herself in the work until she had loosened another mouthful of white fur. Under the intense gaze of the small folk she carried it over to Heath once more. She draped it over his neck, hoping it would help keep him warm.

Behind her, she heard the vines start to rustle. She hopped back to the unicorn. The small folk had surrounded it, and the unicorn was looking understandably apprehensive. She was eyeing down the approaching swarm.

"I think they mean well," Millet assured the unicorn, as well as herself. "I think we just have to trust them." The unicorn remained seated, reluctantly. With one eye on the swarm of small folk Millet returned to the unicorn's side. She resumed tugging at the knotted fur and was not entirely surprised to find small folk climbing the mats beside her to chew the coat in other places. The unicorn shifted uncomfortably as uncounted small furry bodies scurried over it.

"Just let them," Millet suggested, "You need to be free of your fur, don't you?"

"Yes," the unicorn admitted, "but it's been a very long time and I've never been shorn like this. This is not dignified." A pair of small folk had scurried over her forehead and were working away at the fur around the unicorn's eyes.

"I can't believe its happening," Millet said. "Maybe this is magic?"

"If it is, it's terrifying," the unicorn whispered, shutting her eyes to prevent the tails of the small folk dragging across them.

The small folk started to sing.

But there are no bargains here.

The song reminded Millet of the melody the small folk had sung when chewing the ivy, at least initially. As they worked she realised there were more notes and harmonies than before, with increasing levels of complexity. Small folk on different areas of the unicorn, and in different areas of the garden, would sing different melodies at different times, as though calling and answering to each other. They created a beautiful, flowing harmony that was both eerie and hypnotic. To make it even stranger she didn't understand why they did it, or how they knew what to sing. There were no words, only beautiful sound. She wished Stares-at-moon was still here to explain things, or to translate, but she knew wishing wouldn't make it true.

The small folk had even organised themselves into a line to pass down strands and tufts of fur to Heath's resting body and were piling it up around him. *He must be warm under there,* she thought, *I wonder if he can hear them singing. What a sweet lullaby it must be.*

A full moon rose leisurely above the purple vine as Millet and the small folk worked into the night. The labor and the song calmed her mind and her fears. A huge volume of fleece trapped the unicorn and it was steadily being piled around Heath. As she carried another mouthful to him she could only just see his soft brown nose sticking out from the dense covering of fur. She paused to stare at him, but found nothing to say. *Oh, if only the warren Elders could see us now.*

"I must say," the unicorn whispered, so as not to upset the countless small creatures that scurried over her, "you and your little friends seem to be making good progress. I already feel lighter." Much of the shaggy coat had been stripped from her face and chest. Millet could now distinguish the features of her fine head and saw the irregular jagged stump where the second horn should have been. Stares-at-moon had never said anything about a unicorn having two horns. *Perhaps she hadn't been a unicorn before she tried to free the trapped souls,* Millet thought. *Perhaps the wondrous creatures in that book aren't born, but made.*

"I'm glad we can help you," Millet replied, still a little sad. "You're a special creature, even if you can't help us in the way I had hoped." She sat down in front of the unicorn, looking up into the golden eyes. Was it possible the book was wrong? That it hadn't known the unicorn lacked the magic to heal the sick? Or was it simply a lie and the unicorn just another ordinary creature.

"Would you come home with me? You don't have to remain here, haunted by the past, if you don't want to. Back at the warren we knew nothing of They." The unicorn shook her head slowly, forcing some of the small folk to stop their work and hold on, but their song never faltered.

"I may be haunted by my memories, but it's all I have left now. I would rather they be remembered. Who would keep them in their heart, if not me?"

"Rabbits are good with stories," Millet assured her. "We would tell them over and over again, that they might be remembered forever." The unicorn reached down to gently nudge Millet with its dexterous lips.

"I thank you for your offer little one, but I will stay. I'm past changing in my old age." She turned her strong neck to look at the steadily increasing mound of her fur encasing Heath.

"You'll be alright alone," she murmured, "I can tell. You're strong." Millet shook her head.

"I don't think I'll ever be alone," she disagreed. "Not really."

She didn't know how to explain herself properly. Even now, in the purple forest with the unicorn, she imagined what Heath would have said, what he would have thought. His voice was still there in her mind. She imagined her brother sitting next to her, taking in the scene and asking his questions. Part of her didn't believe he was lying deathly still under the white fleece. She fluffed up her own coat as an unexpected chill washed over her.

"Soon you'll be free of your fur," Millet noted, hoping to change the subject. "You'll be able to prance and jump again. Won't that be wonderful?"

"Yes," the unicorn agreed. "I don't know how to thank your little friends." A tail from one of the small folk slipped across the unicorn's left eye, startling her. The white creature did her best to remain still.

"I don't know either," Millet admitted. "I can't understand them. Stares-at-moon did, but it's… not around any more." She thought for a moment.

"They liked the books," she remembered. "They were very excited about the stories inside. Stares-at-moon would read to them. Can you read?"

"I don't know what you mean," the unicorn confessed, chewing her cud once more as the small folk removed itself from her face.

"There were these things called books inside those things," Millet gestured to the abandoned structure at the other end of the meadow. "The books were like a pile of leaves with little markings that told stories. Have you never seen them?"

"I spent little time in those places," the unicorn explained, "and if I did come across something like a pile of leaves, I probably ate it."

"They didn't smell tasty," said Millet. "The small folk don't talk, they only sing, but they listen to stories."

"Oh, little one," the unicorn sighed. "Who says singing isn't talking?" The unicorn stood up slowly, placing her feet with great care around the small folk that tended her. Much of the shaggy, matted white fur that covered her body had been loosened and hung in sheets and tendrils. Most of it was still attached to the creature's underside. The unicorn reached around to her own flank and grabbed a mouthful of fur, small folk climbing quickly out of the way. She tugged with great force until a dense sheet of fleece was torn away from her side.

"Much better," the unicorn mumbled. She dragged her sheet of fleece, small folk still riding on her body, over to where Heath lay hidden in the pile of fur. With the old, outer fleece removed the new fur that remained was even whiter, like the full moon high above them. Despite her age the unicorn looked new again, even with a few tattered tendrils of fur remaining, worked on by the thorough small folk. She shone in the moonlight, surrounded by the walls of purple blooms and the clear night sky. With a flick of her head she tossed the sheet of fleece over the pile covering Heath. It drifted down softly.

Free of her own fur, unicorn suddenly leapt and pranced around the meadow, kicking up her heels and tossing her head for joy. The small folk clung to her, still singing, and picked up their pace. The tone changed. No longer was the melody haunting, but quick and merry. *They must be happy,* Millet thought, *surely they must be happy.* For a brief, blissful moment she forgot herself, and pranced through the grass with the unicorn, freed of her burdens and caught up in the song. The unicorn was such a beautiful creature, shining white and free. It felt good to think that such a little creature like herself had made a difference to something so wonderful. It was a moment of joy, simply joy, until she turned, mid prance, and saw the pile of unicorn fur that concealed her brother's body.

She stopped. The merriment draining from her like sweat as she remembered where she was, and all that had happened to lead her here. How could she be happy now? It wasn't right. She hopped slowly towards her brother, ashamed by her moment of joy. The small folk still sang and the unicorn still pranced, but she no longer felt the song move through her. She felt heavy.

"Brother?" she whispered into the pile of fur, guilty that for a moment she had forgotten about him. "Brother, are you still there?" The pile of fur rustled. Millet's ears pricked up, desperately hoping the noise was one she longed to hear.

A small twitchy nose crept out between the mats of fur, with long whiskers and tiny ears. The small folk glanced at her, brushed a few long white strands out of its face, and joined the quavering song once more. Millet's entire posture sank as it stared at her.

"It's not that I'm not glad you're here," she told the small folk in front of her, "I'd just hoped that you'd be someone else." It skipped from side to side, bouncing in time with the song, as it went to join its brethren in the grass. Millet crouched next to the pile of fur.

"I'm sorry brother, I'm so sorry," she whispered into the fur. "I'm thankful too, of course, but so sorry for you. I'm thankful for the un-rabbit-like thoughts, I wouldn't be here without them, but maybe you would." She sighed to herself and any other soul that might have been listening. The prancing unicorn and the small folk paid her no notice.

"I would give anything for you to be safe and well," the sorrow creeping into her voice was making it harder to speak. She could barely hear herself over the singing and leaping footsteps of the unicorn. "And I know you would have given the same. I just wonder whether you had the opportunity to make the choice, instead of me." She pressed her head against the fur. It gave a little under her weight, but was still warm and smelt of plants. At least Heath would be snug hidden in there.

"I still need you. I want us to go home, together. I'd give anything, anything at all, if you'd wake up. If you'd just come back. Please come back."

Suddenly Millet realised the merry song of the small folk had slowed to a low hum. She stood up; ears erect to listen behind her. Coloured light reflected from the surface of the pond to her side; green, orange and purple. Something was flapping like a dragonfly. Its wings buzzed softly.

She turned her head slowly to look across the meadow.

The unicorn stood perfectly still, sniffing a glowing orb that hovered in front of it. All the small folk stood to attention, each one staring intently at the orb, wherever they were. The orb's three colours, orange, green and purple, flowed around itself, slowly taking a new shape. Cautiously, Millet took a few hops towards it. Nobody else in the meadow seemed to be afraid.

"What is it?" Millet asked as loud as she dared.

"It's a Fey," the unicorn replied. As the creatures watched, the orb of shifting lights grew taller and narrower. The bottom part split into two long legs, though no tail, and distinct gossamer wings fluttered from its back. Two more legs split from the column near the top of its body, leaving a round head. The entire form glowed with the same three shifting colours, bright enough to cast shadows on the grass. Two large black eyes that produced no colour at all dominated its round, flat face. They seemed to suck the light back into them like the depths of the night sky. The creature was only half the size of Millet herself, but its presence felt larger in her mind. It hovered around the unicorn's head, making strange, high-pitched chirping noises. Millet sniffed the air, but the being had no scent.

"What does it want?" she whispered, unwilling to move. The creature hovered towards some of the small folk, bending itself over to touch their noses with its front paws. Its fingers were long and delicate, like Stares-at-moon's had been. The small folk reached up to meet it.

"As far as I can tell," the unicorn replied, sounding rather amused, "It wants to touch heads. They certainly used to." The Fey chirped and chuckled to itself as it spun and danced in the air among the small folk. It then flew away from them, in a haphazard erratic way, as though drifting on a breeze that wasn't there. Millet stared, wide-eyed, as the being caught her gaze.

She wondered if she should run, but it was only a passing thought. The being was mesmerisingly beautiful, like a sweet dream, but Millet was not afraid. She was still cautious, but any proper rabbit would be. It was ethereal, though Millet did not know the word.

"Are you magical?" she whispered to it. The Fey had no words, but continued to click, chuckle and then sing.

It was such a beautiful sound, Millet almost cried for the second time. She felt the song vibrating through her body, in every bone and every hair. It felt like she was floating, but she couldn't break her gaze away from the black eyes of the Fey to check her feet. It was closer now, almost within her reach, just waiting.

"Can you understand me?" she asked it, summoning the courage she had left. The small folk fell silent. Only the Fey itself continued to sing.

"Please, if there's anything you can do, my brother needs help," said Millet. The Fey swayed side to side as it continued to advance. Millet didn't run, but she did lean backwards as the being hovered ever closer. It was so close she saw her own face reflected in its perfectly black eyes, and a tiny mouth below them. The Fey being seemed to occupy the whole world, sucking in light and colour. Nothing else mattered in this moment. It reached forward with one delicate arm, stretched out one long finger, and lightly tapped Millet on the nose.

"Boop!" it sang.

Millet jumped.

The Fey burst into music-like laughter, spun itself backwards and bowed.

"What does it want?" Millet asked anyone that might answer, watching the Fey dance in the air. Her nose felt warm and tingled strangely.

"To touch your head," the unicorn replied softly, "That's all I've ever seen them want." Millet pricked up her ears and sat up straight once more.

"Please, if you can help my brother…" She'd blinked, and the Fey was directly in front of her once more, shifting colours dancing across its face.

"He needs help or he'll…die." The Fey blinked its huge black eyes and touched Millet's nose again.

"Boop!" Millet flinched as it prodded her, a little harder this time. It flipped head over heels laughing and singing as it hovered away, watching Millet with those unreadable black eyes.

"Please, I don't know how to ask you. I'll do anything," Millet cried, "Anything." The Fey spun itself upside down and hovered back to Millet as though its new orientation was not unusual. It hovered just within reach, smiling faintly with its small mouth. It reached out to touch her again. Millet shut her eyes.

Nothing happened.

Slowly Millet dared to look.

The Fey hovered there, finger out stretched, waiting a tiny distance away from Millet's nose. It was completely motionless except for the beating of its gossamer wings. As

Millet studied the creature, she wasn't even sure whether it was breathing. She looked at the finger. She looked at the face of the Fey. It stared back at her, its large eyes devoid of expression. The Fey's entire body was solid, but orange, green and purple blushes of colour flowed across it, including the finger. She looked at the finger again, perfectly still.

The Fey winked.

Millet leaned forward, watching the face cautiously, and slowly pressed her nose against its waiting finger.

"BOOP!" The Fey sang with joy. It clapped and spun in speedy circles around her. It was so fast Millet couldn't keep her eyes on it. Now she was afraid. She felt sick tying to watch it.

Suddenly it shot up into the sky, outlined by the moon. All the animals stared.

"I've never seen them do that before," said the unicorn.

"Is that bad?" Millet asked, afraid to move.

"It's just new." The Fey seemed to glow brighter, whiter. It was as though all the moonlight, all the colours of the garden at night were being dragged into its glowing body. Even the orange fish in the pond seemed grey as the Fey glowed. Millet had to squint as they Fey shone brighter than the moon, brighter than the sun. Its light reflected in the eyes of hoards of uncounted small folk.

The Fey then dropped, falling towards Millet at great speed. It braked just beyond her reach. It was so bright she couldn't make out where its body ended and its light began, but it eyes were still the same untouchable, bottomless black.

Without warning it sped into the pile of unicorn fur that concealed Heath.

Your dreams shall be different till the
day you die.

"No!" Millet gasped. The whole pile of fur glowed with the Fey's three hued light. Millet ran up to it, but didn't dare touch it.

"Brother!" she wailed. The glowing pile pulsed and throbbed

rapidly. Heat radiated from it, like the harsh heat of the flames.

"There's nothing you can do," said the unicorn, walking up behind her. Millet stared, full of worry, from between the unicorn's feet. Silence fell and the singing vanished, from both the Fey and the small folk. The pulses of light slowed and faded.

"I don't know where it's gone," Millet whispered.

"I think it's still here," said the unicorn, far too calm in Millet's opinion, "though they do often vanish without a trace." The pile of fur only glowed faintly now, and colour seemed to return to the world. The silence slowly filled with the distant chirp of crickets as the glow faded completely from the pile of fur.

"What an eventful evening," the unicorn noted placidly, as though nothing miraculous had occurred.

Millet froze and listened hard. She wasn't convinced the Fey had gone. Perhaps it was her imagination, but she thought something moved within the pile.

There was a faint scurrying behind her as the small folk went about their business, whatever that may be. Clearly their excitement was over.

Millet pricked up her ears. She was certain something had moved in the pile. She didn't know what kind of game the Fey thought it was playing, but it wasn't a very funny one.

The pile of unicorn fur, complete with all the tangled plant material, was piled almost as tall as the unicorn itself. It was quite heavy, but Millet saw no entry where the Fey might have burrowed into it. Perhaps a creature like the Fey was not concerned with such things. She boldly hopped forward to the pile and began sniffing it. The creature had no scent before, and the odor of the fur was still overwhelmingly the unicorn's with the occasional hint of rotting plant.

And the tiniest hint of a very familiar rabbit.

Would the Fey help him? Or would it just play more games? Millet had no idea, and suddenly, urgently, wanted to lay eyes on her brother, just to know he was still there. Did a creature as strange as the Fey have any concept of what she meant?

She nuzzled through the fur, parting clumps as she tried to work her way into the centre of the pile, tried to find her brother. She buried her head in the soft fur and prickly stems. It muffled sound, she couldn't hear anything behind or in front of her. She couldn't see very far and the unicorn musk on the fur was becoming overpowering. She sensed nothing but the soft, close fur and her rapidly beating heart. Her breath barely moved from the space in front of her. She wondered if it was possible to suffocate in there.

Her claws grabbed the fur, but rather than shift it they tracked through it, stretching it in different directions but making little progress. *How had the unicorn even walked carrying this around,* she wondered, *no wonder she jumped for joy.*

Something definitely moved ahead of her, rustling through the fur. Strong, deliberate movements pushed towards her.

She paused, her mind needing time to think before her body responded to instinct. Heath was in here, but in no state to move. There were small folk here, but unless they were all moving in unison then whatever was ahead of her was simply too big.

Then there was the Fey. Who knew what it might do?

In any case restricting her vision and movement in the pile of fur was a foolish thing to do. She wiggled backwards rapidly, flashing her tail out in the cool night air. Her hind feet gripped the grass below her, and she finally had traction to move herself out. She scampered a few paces away from the pile and turned back to watch from a safe distance. Clumps of fluff had stuck to her fur, and she quickly brushed them from her whiskers. The unicorn lowered its head to her level, taking care not to strike her with its horn, also sniffing the air. "I don't know what's happening," Millet admitted.

"We rarely do, truly," the unicorn advised her, "but you will have to find out sooner or later." The thing moving in the fur was distinctly closer, tufts of fleece fell away as whatever waited there disturbed the layers beneath them.

"I suspect sooner," the unicorn added. Millet took a deep breath. She hopped forward slowly, stopping after each pace to listen to the pile of fur. The air felt oddly empty without the singing of the small folk even though it was no different than when she had entered the meadow. If only the fur didn't muffle the sound so much she might know what to expect. She had faced many new things in the last few days, but none were so deeply frightening now she did not have her brother by her side.

She forced herself forward until she was standing next to the pile once more. The source of the movement was barely concealed, she almost convinced herself she could see it. Whatever it was, it certainly took its time freeing itself. *I can't sit here worrying all night,* Millet told herself, and let fear give way to curiosity. She reached forward, grabbed a large clump of fur in her teeth, and flung it behind her.

She looked back at the mound.

A nose was visible, clearly a rabbit's nose with twitching rabbit's whiskers, but as white as the unicorn itself. It was as white as Stares-at-moon's face had been, as white as the moon.

Millet scampered backwards, heart thumping, until she backed into the legs of the unicorn. She looked up at her new, white fur towering over her. *What if stories are wrong,* she wondered, *what if it's not a horn?* She reminded herself that she had to be brave. Frightened rabbits ran, brave rabbits had a chance to learn.

She hopped forward again, faster this time, and watched the creature trying to free itself. She leaned in and flicked away another clump of leaf-ridden fur.

Red eyes stared back at her. Their pupil was the colour of blood, even under the moon, but the iris a paler pink like the eyelid's skin. They stared at her from a rabbit's face devoid of colour.

Heath's face.

"What are you?" Millet whispered. The white rabbit shook his head, freeing his ears from the fur encasing him. He considered the question for a time Millet thought longer than strictly necessary.

"Enlightened," he said at last. It was certainly Heath's voice, Heath's shape, but not a spot of Heath's colour remained.

"Also, alive," he added. Millet tried to sniff him, tried to pick out a familiar scent, but the musk from the unicorn fur was still too potent.

"Is it really you, brother?" she asked. The white rabbit cocked his head to one side, ears swiveling to face her.

"What an odd question. Who else would I be?"

"I think perhaps you need to look at yourself with new eyes," suggested the unicorn. The white rabbit looked the unicorn up and down.

"So that's what you look like," he said, "I could hear you, though I think I was very far away. It is a privilege to finally meet you." The unicorn stood a little straighter and puffed out her chest. The white rabbit pulled itself from the pile of fur and stretched. He looked every inch like Heath, but free of the swellings of his sickness and completely white, save for his red eyes. He shook himself from nose to tail, dislodging the sparse unicorn hairs that still clung to him. They were difficult to see, practically the same colour as his coat.

"The water will show you," the unicorn suggested, gesturing to the pool beside her. Millet and the white rabbit shared a glance before she led him to the pool. The orange fish floated lazily near the surface until it sensed their approach and darted into the depths. Its tail caused ripples on the surface, distorting the rabbits' reflections. They both peered at the waters, waiting for them to settle.

"So you heard the unicorn," Millet wondered, "What else?"

"Not much else," replied the white rabbit, "but I was glad you found her. I thought she said she couldn't help me?"

"I couldn't," the unicorn replied. The white rabbit stood on his hind legs, bringing his face as close as possible to the unicorn.

"Then how am I standing here?" Millet glanced at the silent unicorn. Her expression gave nothing away.

"You don't remember hearing anything else?" Millet asked. The white rabbit shook his head.

"No," he replied, glancing at the settling water. Millet cocked her head to one side. *How could he not have heard the small folk singing?* She had felt their voices in her bones, surely he would have heard them in the pile of fur? Some of them had even been in the pile themselves.

Of course, there is another possibility, Millet thought to herself. *He may not have been here to hear them.* She couldn't think of a good way to answer him. She wasn't even sure yet that it was Heath standing before her. He looked so unnatural all in white.

As if he sensed her uncertainty, the white rabbit lowered himself and brought himself nose to nose with her. Their whiskers brushed against each other, and at last his scent filled her nostrils. He smelled just like her brother, even if his colours were gone.

The water settled. The white rabbit leaned over the edge and peered at his reflection. He turned his head slowly from side to side, peering at the red-eyed, white-furred reflection in front of him. Millet hopped up to the edge as well. A small brown rabbit stared back at her from the water's surface, perfectly mirroring her actions.

"I am… different," he said at last. "No wonder you didn't recognise me." He continued to turn his head in this way and that, inspecting his face as much as the water would allow.

"I have the eyes of Stares-at-moon," he marveled at himself.

He rubbed his paws along his eyes and ears.

"I feel great," he said. "Full of energy. Light." As if to prove it he began to bounce and race around the meadow, prancing, bounding, shaking himself mid leap. He laughed. She had to admit, his energy was infectious. He seemed happier than she ever remembered her brother being. That was, if the creature before her was still her brother, or only her brother. There was no sign of the Fey.

Had he really not heard the singing? Not heard the Fey? And where had the Fey gone? For that matter, where had it come from?

As she watched the white rabbit prance in the moonlight, shimmering before her, she wondered whether it mattered. What would she not have offered the Fey for it to bring her brother back to her? What would he have traded for his own life? Was colour really such a big price?

Did it matter? He was here now. He smelled like her brother, he sounded like her brother, even looked like him except for one obvious difference. Would it really matter what colour he was if they travelled under cover and kept to shelter? He was so white, he'd be blinding in the midday sun.

She turned to the unicorn, also watching the white rabbit prance and shake around the grass. They were just as white as each other. *Maybe that's how it works,* she wondered, *maybe the white is the mark of the unicorn.*

Or of the Fey.

But if it meant having her brother back, what wouldn't she have given up? What was colour worth, really?

Her brother was here.

She leapt into the grass with him, prancing and shaking, fluffing herself up. They chased each other around the meadow, playing like they had as kits. The unicorn bleated and joined in their chase. They played and pranced for joy under the clear light of the moon, two white bodies and one brown.

When at last they settled, tired but glad of it, the rabbits curled up by the unicorn's flanks under the purple vine. They dozed lightly to the sound of her churning stomach as she chewed her cud. They didn't feel frightened because they didn't feel exposed. The meadow was safe, now they were together once more. They drifted in and out of sweet dreams until the hint of dawn brushed the sky.

Millet seized the opportunity to feast on the sweet grass around them while the unicorn dozed in the early morning. Her brother joined her, and she was pleased to see him eat hungrily, something he hadn't done for days. It was strange to see him with the white fur and red eyes though, as if part of him wasn't quite there.

"I am here," he said softly between mouthfuls, as though he knew what she had been thinking.

"Yes," she replied, "I… I know, but I don't think I actually believed." He paused his meal to wash his paws and face, cleaning the succulent grass juices from his fur.

"You must have believed," he assured her warmly. "After all, you got us both here. If you hadn't believed, I would have shut these eyes of mine elsewhere, and never opened them again." Millet considered this. Of course she believed then, with all her heart. Why was it that now, with her brother standing before her, well and vigorous, that her belief faltered? Were these un-rabbit-like thoughts again? Come to think of it, when was the last time she had a definitely rabbit thought? She shook her fur at the notion, madness surely lay that way.

"I don't think I believed," Heath told her, "but I find myself understanding so much more now. I have a sense… it's like I can hear extra things, but it's not with my ears. And I have the eyes of Stares-at-moon, I wonder if they will let me understand the books, to see what it saw. We must find them again." Millet grew cautious. While it certainly sounded like her brother speaking, the desire to not go home was new. She wasn't sure it was such a good thing.

"No," she said, "we need to return to the warren. We need to find the Great Eucalypt, or what's left of it." Her brother looked like he was ready to argue, but she wasn't about to let him.

"If anyone else survived, they will need help. More ears, more eyes, more diggers. We cannot forget them just because they are out of sight, nor can we forget that we are rabbits and we need our warren. The books have waited a long time, they can wait a bit longer. Our warren may not be able to." She watched him bite back the words he had been thinking and consider her point.

"You've always had un-rabbit-like thoughts," she continued, "We both have. They didn't understand them and didn't want them in the days when life was simple and good for us. But the days aren't simple anymore. It may be that now is the time when the warren needs new thoughts, thoughts like ours, like yours, more than it ever has before." Heath considered her words carefully, chewing slowly on a long blade of grass. Millet waited for an answer, wondering to herself whether she really would go home without him if it came down to it.

"We're not like other rabbits," he said at last, "We're not even like ourselves when we were first washed through the stone burrow. We are different. The world is the same, but it is we who have changed." He gestured to the abandoned structure at one end of the meadow.

"I hear, and I know, that thing was called a house. This place is its garden. They lived in it, and They were called man. I have grown wise to this and I don't understand how." He turned back to his sister, listening worriedly.

"You, little Millet have grown fierce in the defense of others, even me. That bravery is new in you."

He waved a paw at the dozing unicorn the early dawn light.

"I hear, though not with my ears, that the creature you call a unicorn is in fact called a goat. At least, she was in the days before the dust, but she may also still be a unicorn. I conceive of no reason why a creature could not be many things at once. The dryad, the dragon, the small folk and the long tail all have other names as well. I can hear them if I focus very hard, but that does not mean the whispers are more true than the words already spoken." Millet stared at the unicorn, or goat, or whatever name she was supposed to be known by. Whatever the word was it didn't make the creature any less special, no more or less magical, then she had been the moment she first set eyes upon her.

"But I know nothing of the dust, or the day that it fell," Heath continued, beginning to sound worried. "And as much as having this knowledge in the first place troubles me, it is the missing pieces that trouble me more." At least that was one thing Millet could understand. It was like finding silence when you expected a sound. It meant something was wrong. The unicorn, or goat, snorted and awoke at the sound of her own noise. She surveyed the meadow, or garden, and finding everything to be how she remembered wandered over to the pool for a drink. Millet hopped towards it, followed shortly by her brother. It may be some time before they had a good opportunity to drink again.

"Your garden is lovely," Heath told the unicorn. "The grass is fresh and it's delightfully cool. Everywhere else has been so hot of late."

"Yes," the unicorn murmured. "It's always spring here. I think the Fey like it."

"Unicorn," Millet asked shyly, almost appologetically, "I didn't ask you properly before, but what do you prefer to be called? I believe you are a unicorn, but Heath thinks you used to be called goat. What is your name, truly? I'm sorry I never asked before." The unicorn stared down at her quizzically.

"I am what I am," she said, "and I always will be. However in the days before the dust fell They would call me Cuddles."

"So you're a Cuddles?"

"As I understood it, that was my name, my who, not my what. Not that it matters greatly, any name you would give me is fine."

"Noble Cuddles," said Heath, rising on his hind legs with as much respectability as he could muster. Millet had to admit that he did look more authoritative than be used to and wondered how the warren elders that had survived would react. "Will you please show us our way home, guide us from these paths you roam? While we have not been away from home very long, much has changed within ourselves, but I fear what may have changed at our warren."

"I can guide you towards the the lightning strikes," replied Cuddles. "That is as far as I know. From there you will have to find your way alone."

"In the end, we always travel alone, but we thank you for the right direction," Heath replied.

There are no happy endings, for nothing ends.

Cuddles, the unicorn, guided them through the maze of abandoned houses and gardens along the black and pale grey stone paths that Heath declared were called roads. Cuddles walked quite happily out in the open. She had no fear of death from the skies above, nor of being seen. She sometimes led them through shade, but more often than not would contentedly drift through open spaces. The shining new white coat provided no camouflage at all, though Millet wondered whether the white fur would have helped her hide in any sort of cover.

"Aren't you afraid something will see you and want to eat you?" Millet asked her as Cuddles led them to a particularly tasty bush for a moment's rest.

"Not anymore," Cuddles replied with a mouthful of leaves. "I'm far too big for any of the birds to take while I can still walk, and the nasty howlers cleared out long ago. I've not heard their howls or barks for a few summers now. No little one, the only creatures here that would eat me now will wait until I'm dead."

"Don't you feel exposed out in the open?" Millet asked. Cuddles chuckled.

"I'm too big to hide well, and without my leaves I do stand out." Millet had to admit Cuddles had a point. She wondered how Heath would manage to hide near the warren. He lacked the protection of the unicorn's size, and there was almost certainly a vengeful hawk waiting for them.

For his part, Heath wasn't paying them much attention. The white rabbit sat in the shade from the bush, eyes closed but ears swiveling in different directions. Sometimes his whole head would twitch towards something and he would sniff the air, but Millet had no idea what he was hearing or sensing. She only heard songbirds and blowflies, and surely they weren't that interesting. As she grazed nearby she kept one eye on him and one eye on their surroundings. The unicorn might feel safe and untouchable, but she certainly didn't. Her brother seemed to be increasingly upset by whatever it was he was listening to.

She hopped towards him and nudged his ears gently until he opened his pink eyes.

"What is it you hear?" she asked him. He opened his eyes, red pupils constricting against the bright midday light.

"I'm listening to everything," he breathed. "There is so much noise in this place. The noise is so old." Millet stood up and listened as hard as she could. The buzzing of flies and the rustle of leaves reached her ears. She could even hear the breeze through the houses, and their own breath, but it wasn't what she would consider lots of noise. She didn't understand what he meant by a noise being old either. Even echoes were transient.

"I can hear Them walking, talking, living. There's so many! And then it just stops. Silence."

"Silence?"

"Yes," Heath replied, "Silence. They just vanish. I think that's when the dust fell. But they don't scream, there's no change in the activity, they just fall silent." Millet looked around.

"It's quiet now," she told him.

"Yes, and I don't know why." He seemed unusually bothered by something that wasn't a threat to them. She sighed.

"I think I need to tell you about last night, and the Fey."

Heath listened in silence as Millet retold the events he had missed from the previous night. His pink eyes grew wide as she told him about the Fey, pupils the colour of blood. She'd never liked the colour much anyway, but it was deeply unsettling having it as a permanent part of her brother's face. She supposed she'd have to get used to it.

"There is too much to know," he said at last. "Too much to listen to, too much to think about."

"Does it actually change the here and now?" Millet asked him. She had no idea what he was thinking but the important thing was to keep them both safe. Heath had spent far less thoughts on keeping himself alive than he normally would. Then again, maybe he'd seen the alternative. Maybe it didn't worry him anymore.

"No" he said to her great relief, "I need to get back to the warren. I need to know if I can hear them there. I need time to understand what's going on."

"So we go home," Millet told him.

"Yes," Heath agreed, "but one day, we'll come back." He hopped away towards the waiting unicorn. "But I'm not planning on swimming next time!" he added.

Millet tried to remember the landmarks they passed but so many things looked and smelled the same she would never be able to remember the way back. Heath, by contrast, took to reading marks on the ground and on leafless trees with single short, flat branches at the top.

"It's how They would navigate," he'd said, which was news to Cuddles as well. "Not with scent, but with words on all sorts of things."

"You can read them?" She had been surprised, but this revelation had been far from the most surprising thing she had dealt with lately.

"It's the red eyes of Stares-at-moon," he said, "I think that's how. They just make sense in my head."

"That's… strange," Millet replied, perplexed. Heath sighed

and scratched an ear.

"You have no idea."

The houses became sparser and the plants more familiar in the days that the unicorn led them back towards their home. Millet was glad to see them even if the grasses were dry and not quite as sweet as those from the gardens. Cuddles lead them across short grassland to the edge of a forest, surrounded by a firm mesh, hot to touch in the sun. Heath called it a fence.

"This is as far as I can take you," said Cuddles. "I saw the storm clouds beyond here. The rest is up to you."

"How do we get through the fence?" Heath asked. "The holes are much too small."

"I would have thought you'd relish the chance to dig under," the unicorn laughed, "But if that's no longer your taste, allow me." Cuddles lowered her head and hooked her horn through one of the links. She tugged and pulled until the fence curled up from the ground, leaving just enough space for a rabbit to squeeze under. Heath wiggled through, the bottom of the fence combing across his back and catching tufts of white fur. Millet went to follow, but paused. The unicorn's head was at her eye level, horn hooked onto the wire, big golden eyes watching her.

"Thank you," she said, pressing her nose against the long white muzzle. "For everything you've done, and anything you couldn't, but happened anyway. Thank you." She scurried under the lifted fence and the unicorn untangled herself, somewhat ungracefully.

"Farewell small ones," Cuddles called after them as they hopped into the undergrowth, "Farewell!"

The undergrowth of the forest was cool and shaded, but Millet found herself missing the comfort of travelling with the unicorn and her complete lack of fear. Many smells were familiar, but they were not comforting either. There was definitely the scent of a fox, a few days old, making her nose sting.

Heath seemed calmer surrounded by the trees, despite the scent of the cunning predator.

"There are less voices here," he said after travelling under the trees for only a few minutes.

"Is that good?" Millet asked him.

"I don't know," he replied. She laughed.

"Well at least some things about you never change. You might have become enlightened to a whole new way of seeing the world, but you still don't know anything!" He laughed as well. It was good to hear.

"Indeed. I understand so much more than I did, but what I understand most is the sheer amount of things I do not understand, that I didn't even imagine before." He glanced up at the sky with awe even though it was completely obscured by the trees. "It's like my mind is the sky. It used to be night with only the light of the moon and a few twinkling stars for ideas. Now it is day and there is so much more light, more understanding, in my mind. I can hardly know where to begin."

"I know exactly where to begin," Millet reminded him. "We go back to the warren and see what has happened there."

"Yes," he agreed, "I just get so caught up with what's in my head that I forget the rest of me."

"Well you put one foot in front of the other and keep moving," Millet urged him. "Somewhere in this direction is home." *And somewhere around here will be a fox,* she thought to herself. She wanted to tell him it wouldn't be anything in his mind that got him killed, but his inattention to their surroundings. She had been keeping watch for both of them, just as she had when he was sick. Now that he seemed well it felt unfair to be doing the surveillance for both of them.

The forest gave way rather suddenly to grassland, and Millet could see long stretches of terrain ahead of them. Clear skies offered no clouds to shelter them from the sun. The scent of burnt plants drifted past on the breeze. Surely that was a good sign, in a bad way. The long grasses had burned, leaving very little ground cover, though a few charred stumps of scraggly trees remained. Most of the ash underfoot had been washed away, but there was still enough to stick to their fur as they tracked through it. Millet scanned the sky for hawks, and she was pleased to see her brother start to do the same. *Maybe there's still enough proper rabbit thoughts left,* she thought, *or maybe he remembers the wound far too well.*

The ash that remained stuck to his white fur, colouring most of his lower half grey, almost to the point of looking natural. She wondered if there was any point in trying to conceal his new colour, covering him in dust and ash each day. She realised it probably wouldn't last and would wash off as soon as he got wet. In any case she could think of no way to hide his eyes. *What are the Elders going to say?*

Small green shoots erupted through the ash in many places, tentatively reaching towards the sky. Here and there, even burnt trees sprouted a few hopeful leaves. The landscape wanted to live, was starting to recover. It gave her hope for the warren. She hadn't considered before now that even if others survived what would they have left to eat? How would they have managed to feed themselves these last few days? Was it possible that she and her brother had taken the easiest path to survival, despite everything they'd faced?

"I've been thinking," Heath said to her as they struggled up a hill. Millet jerked as a small skink darted for cover in her peripheral vision. She was glad some of them had survived.

"You've been thinking a lot," she reminded him. Millet didn't have a concept of sarcasm, but that didn't mean she couldn't use it on occasion.

"Thinking about us, I mean. What we are."

"We're rabbits," Millet told him, "and that's not as complicated an idea as you make it out to be."

"But we're more than that," Heath insisted, trudging up the slope.

"Yes," Millet agreed, "We're listeners, runners, diggers. We're survivors, and we're thinkers. We are all those things, but we are still, at our core, rabbits."

"I wouldn't dispute any of that," said Heath. He sat down in a small patch of shade from a charred bush and attempted to articulate the thoughts that had clearly been bouncing around his head for some time.

"But 'rabbit' is the skin we wear. It's not our core, not our heart." Millet sighed at her brother. She had nothing against the un-rabbit-like thoughts, she'd had them herself, but was developing a persistent skepticism about them when they got in the way of living. How could he possibly convince himself that a rabbit was not a rabbit?

"Then what are we?" she demanded with the faintest hint of anger sneaking into her tone. She was embarrassed as soon as the words came out. She hadn't meant to be angry, but she was becoming frustrated with her brother's lack of focus on the world around them.

"What was never identified in the book?" Heath asked, but continued before Millet had a chance to think, let alone answer him. "What gains the dragon's wisdom, only if it is brave and can outwit the beast? What is fooled by the dryad? Even the unicorn, remember in the book? If they are true and brave and never falter, if they are brave and pure of heart then the unicorn will appear to them." Heath was clearly growing excited as he talked though Millet was unsure why.

"Appear to what?" Millet demanded, not following her brother's rant or riddle. Would all their days be like this now?

"Appear to heroes!" Heath declared excitedly. "For that is what we are! Our skin may be those of rabbits, but our cores are those of heroes." Millet cocked her head and stared at her brother. The idea clearly grabbed him but Millet was unsure of its significance.

"And what do heroes do?" she asked him, trying to sound more patient. She had always been able to rely on him in the past, but now he was distracted and less predictable. It wasn't just his fur that had changed.

"Heroes do anything that would frighten anyone else," Heath

declared, "They face dragons and find unicorns. They go on great journeys and accomplish impossible things, and when they come home again at last they are different, because their story has changed them." He spoke with a concerning amount of conviction, but Millet did have to admit that it sounded like they had done the things that heroes do.

"The voices speak of many heroes," Heath continued, reverent of the sounds only he could hear. "I hear… bits and pieces when I try to listen. There are so many heroes and I've only just begun to understand them. There's Robin Hood, Hercules and Jason. There's something called a Mandela, and a Spartacus. There's Thor, Ned Kelly, the Swagman, and Peter, Briar, and Hazel… so many, many names. So many stories and not enough time to understand them all."

"So you think we're heroes," said Millet tiredly. "I'm pretty sure we're both still rabbits. More importantly I'm sure we'll be something's meal if we don't keep going."

It was hard not to leave tracks in the burnt soil. As much as the ash had stuck to them they in turn had left a fine trail of footprints behind them. There wasn't much she could do about it now though.

"I don't think there's any reason we can't be both," Heath insisted enthusiastically. "I mean, take yourself for example. Now you are my sister. One day you'll become a mother, but you'll never stop being my sister. Why can't a rabbit become a hero if she is brave and cunning and true?"

"I suppose you might be right," Millet conceded, though she didn't really consider herself as a hero, just the same Millet she had always been. *But am I really,* she mused. *I've faced fire and flood, the unknown and the small folk. I did outwit the dragon, and I did find the unicorn.* She watched her brother scratch a particularly difficult spot behind his ears, leaving marks of grey ash. *Perhaps I saved him too,* she thought, *as much as he saved me to start with.*

"And we have changed on this journey, as heroes are inclined to do," Heath continued. Millet suspected he would continue talking all day if she let him, and she really wanted to find water if they had the chance. The tiny green shoots, only a few days old, were succulent, but scant, and the heat of the day was draining to travel through. She would be glad to be home but had to admit there were benefits to living in the unicorn's home, particularly when it came to finding water. She continued up the hill, hoping her brother would get the hint and follow her. Otherwise, she supposed she would have to come back for him to stop him talking to himself.

"I am no longer just Heath," he said, hurrying to catch up to her. "And you're no longer just little Millet."

"Oh? So what are we then?" She tried to listen carefully over the hill and paid less attention to her brother. It was downwind to them, and she didn't know what may wait on the other side. They had come a long way and faced so much, to be ambushed now would be simply unacceptable.

"You are brave of heart," Heath told her. "You reached out to the small folk and faced down the dragon. When I was failing you set out on your own, not for your benefit, but for mine. You must have been brave to find the unicorn at all, let alone to face what happened afterwards. You are Millet, the Braveheart."

"Am I now?" she chuckled, working her way up the ash laden slopes.

"Indeed," Heath insisted, "and that is how stories will remember you, all the tales of Fey that will be told."

"And what about you, brother?" she asked, bemused.

"I have become wise to the way of man," he told her. "I understand their words and hear their voices. There is so much I don't yet know but now I am aware of my own ignorance."

"So you are Heath, the ignorant?" Millet joked.

"I would prefer Heath the Wise of Man, or the Wiseman, for simplicity. That it how the stories will remember me."

"Okay Wiseman," Millet joked, "we still have a way to go." She reached the top of the hill and stared. Charred grasslands stretched away in from of them, and on the horizon, barely able to distinguish it, was the charred frame of a Great Eucalypt tree.

"Could that be…" Millet's voice trailed off as she dared to hope.

"Home," Heath finished for her. "I dare say we might be there by dusk if we're fast."

"How's your leg?" Millet asked cheekily. Heath thumped boldly on the ground with no hesitation.

"As good as it's ever been!" he declared. "Possibly better!" Millet pranced on the spot, itching to run now home was so close.

"I'll race you!" she declared, bouncing on the spot.

"You're on!"

The rabbits raced across the burnt grasslands, darting

around stumps of charcoal and scorched rocks. Skinks startled and skittered out of the way, peering back from their shelters to watch the rabbits tearing past. Fortunately that seemed to be all there was watching them. Heath's entire back shone white in the afternoon sun, his entire body like a warning flash of a tail. Millet kept up with him, a feat she never would have managed before. The two rabbits paced each other in their game. The black skeleton of the burnt Eucalypt grew larger on the horizon as they approached.

Millet skidded to a halt. Her brother stopped a second after her, turning back to see why she had stopped.

"Tired?" he teased. She ignored him, sniffing the soil in front of her. There was a pile of scat left here, still fairly fresh. They would have burnt, fibrous as they were. They had to be fresh. That had to mean somebody was still around here. That had to mean somebody survived.

She inspected the pile a little closer. A couple of somebodies most likely.

"Some survived," she whispered to her brother, barely able to believe it herself.

"Come on," he urged her. "Let's go see."

They slowed their pace as they approached the Eucalypt. Millet was sure it was their tree, and her confidence only grew as familiar scents mingled with the surrounding ash. Looking ahead, she could even see where the first branch had fallen in the fire. It had to be home.

They slowed down as they reached the base of the hill where the Eucalypt grew. Millet listened intently for a sign of any survivors that might still be there. While there were many fresh green shoots peeking through the burnt plants, they were measly mouthfuls at best.

A warning was thumped on the ground up ahead. Anxiously, Millet looked around for the danger. Somebody thumped again. She couldn't see what to they were warning for.

"I think it's me," Heath whispered beside her. "I don't think they know what I am." *Was that all*, Millet wondered.

"Come on then," she decided. "Let's show them you're nothing to be afraid of."

"Oh, but I'm something new," Heath argued, "and new things are always feared. At least until they're not new."

"Then let's get you up there. We've got a story to tell."

Millet bounded up the hill to the base of the Eucalypt where half a dozen rabbits braced he themselves to sprint into their burrows and bolt holes.

"Don't be afraid!" she called out. "It's only us! We've come home!" She could tell they were staring at Heath behind her and reminded herself how strange he must look to them.

"Millet?" A young buck hopped forward, sniffing cautiously. She recognised him as a recent visitor to the warren by the name of Bracken.

"Yes!" she called out, "And Heath too! We're home!" Bracken hopped forward, sniffing her and then her brother as though he didn't quite believe they were standing there in front of him.

"What happened to you," he asked at last. The other rabbits crept forward a few steps themselves, peering cautiously at Heath, his white coat and red eyes.

"Now that," said Heath, the Wiseman, "is quite a story. Let us tell you from the beginning."

Afterword

The lives of animals are closely entwined with our own. They have fascinated us from our earliest memories, and I believe will continue to do so for as long as we coexist together. I have often wondered whether we might fascinate them in the same way.

The Big Ears Animal Sanctuary in Longford, Tasmania, provides a permanent home for hundreds of rescued or surrendered animals. My personal experience is that all the inhabitants there are treated with care and compassion. Despite difficulties faced by the humans of the sanctuary, they have continued to provide a safe home and excellent care for so many animals, including chickens, roosters, turkeys, cats, livestock, guinea pigs and, of course, countless rabbits.

I would urge you to visit their websites and offer them support.

Thank you for reading.

http://www.bigearsanimalsanctuary.com/

https://www.facebook.com/bigears.sanctuary

Endnotes

Epigraph chapter titles quotes are from the following novels:

"When men are fairy tales in books written by rabbits," *The Last Unicorn,* Peter S Beagle, Viking press 1968

"But first they must catch you," *Watership Down,* Richard Adams, Rex Collings 1972

"Take me with you stream, far, far away," *Watership Down,* Richard Adams, Rex Collings 1972

"Uncertainty itself was the worst suffering," *Mrs Firsby and the Rats of NIMH,* Robert C. O'Brien, Antheneum 1971

"We were ordinary street rats," *Mrs Firsby and the Rats of NIMH,* Robert C. O'Brien, Antheneum 1971

"They passed down all the roads long ago," *The Last Unicorn,* Peter S Beagle, Viking press 1968

"Listen. Don't listen to me, just listen," *The Last Unicorn,* Peter S Beagle, Viking press 1968

"I will keep the colour of your eyes," *The Last Unicorn,* Peter S Beagle, Viking press 1968

"We are not always what we seem," *The Last Unicorn,* Peter S Beagle, Viking press 1968

"And hardly ever what we dream," *The Last Unicorn,* Peter S Beagle, Viking press 1968

"Be cunning and full of tricks," *Watership Down,* Richard Adams, Rex Collings 1972

"Why must you always speak in riddles," *The Last Unicorn,* Peter S Beagle, Viking press 1968

"The first primroses were beginning to bloom," *Watership Down,* Richard Adams, Rex Collings 1972

"If you are human enough to cry no magic in the world can change you back," *The Last Unicorn,* Peter S Beagle, Viking press 1968

"The unicorn lived in a lilac wood, and she lived all alone," *The Last Unicorn,* Peter S Beagle, Viking press 1968

"But there are no bargains here," *Watership Down,* Richard Adams, Rex Collings 1972

"Your dreams shall be different till the day you die," *The Last Unicorn,* Peter S Beagle, Viking press 1968

"There are no happy endings, for nothing ends," *The Last Unicorn,* Peter S Beagle, Viking press 1968

Upcoming Novels

Fables Written By Rabbits – Coming Soon!

The warren is shocked when a black rabbit is born in their midst. Is she an omen of ill fortune, or simply of change? When a star falls from the sky, Heath, Millet and her young family decide to seek it out, hoping for answers about mankind and the Fey.

But there are new dangers and challenges waiting for them. A pack of desperate dogs will do anything for one more meal, and the tricky cat knows very different stories of mankind, that Heath can hardly believe.

For updates about this and other upcoming books, please join us online.

You can find us at www.FeroxPublishing.com and join our mailing list to stay up to date.

Or join us on Facebook by searching Ferox Publishing.

You can also contact the author on Twitter @DrFerox